FIREHAND

Tor books by Andre Norton

Caroline (with Enid Cushing)
The Crystal Gryphon
Dare to Go A-Hunting
The Elvenbane (with Mercedes Lackey)
Empire of the Eagle (with Susan Shwartz)
Flight in Yiktor
Forerunner
Forerunner: The Second Venture
Gryphon's Eyrie (with A. C. Crispin)
Grand Masters' Choice (editor)
Here Abide Monsters
House of Shadows (with Phyllis Miller)
Imperial Lady (with Susan Shwartz)
The Jekyll Legacy (with Robert Bloch)
Moon Called
Moon Mirror
The Prince Commands
Ralestone Luck
Redline the Stars (with P. M. Griffin)
Sneeze on Sunday (with Grace Allen Hogarth)
Songsmith (with A. C. Crispin)
Stand and Deliver
Wheel of Stars
Wizards' Worlds
Wraiths of Time

TALES OF THE WITCH WORLD (editor)

Tales of the Witch World 1
Tales of the Witch World 2
Four from the Witch World
Tales of the Witch World 3

WITCH WORLD: THE TURNING

Storms of Victory (with P. M. Griffin)
Flight of Vengeance (with P. M. Griffin and Mary H. Schaub)
On Wings of Magic (with Patricia Mathews and Sasha Miller)

MAGIC IN ITHKAR (editor, with Robert Adams)

Magic in Ithkar 1
Magic in Ithkar 2
Magic in Ithkar 3
Magic in Ithkar 4

FIREHAND

ANDRE NORTON
& P. M. GRIFFIN

19672

813
NOR

TOR

A TOM DOHERTY ASSOCIATES BOOK   NEW YORK

FIREHAND

This book is printed on acid-free paper.

Edited by James Frenkel

A Tor Book
Published by Tom Doherty Associates, Inc.
175 Fifth Avenue
New York, N.Y. 10010

Tor ® is a registered trademark of Tom Doherty Associates, Inc.

Library of Congress Cataloging-in-Publication Data

Norton, Andre.
    Firehand / Andre Norton and P.M. Griffin.
        p.   cm.
    "A Tom Doherty Associates book."
    ISBN 0-312-85313-0
        1. Imaginary wars and battles—Fiction.   2. Time travel—Fiction.
    I. Griffin, P. M. (Pauline M.)   II. Title.
    PS3527.O632F53   1994
    813'.52—dc20   94-604
                                                                          CIP

First edition: June 1994

Printed in the United States of America

0 9 8 7 6 5 4 3 2 1

For my Uncle, Patrick Murphy,
who taught me how to build round towers.
—P.M.G.

FIREHAND

1

ROSS MURDOCK'S EYES flickered to the dancing flames of the small fire he had made. Fire. The ancient symbol of home and hearth. The source of warmth and light. Humanity's ally against the dark and the things, real and imagined, that haunted it. Man's friend. Man's enemy. Fire could hurt, too, as evidenced by his scorched face and hands.

Even in that, it was his aide. Pain, clean physical agony, cut through the chain of mental compulsion with which the starmen were attempting to bind and draw him to their will.

Anger flickered inside him, leaping up like the tongues of his fire. The aliens had hunted him for days now, followed him inexorably as he had struggled downriver in his desperate effort to reach this rendezvous point. They had sought him, and they had turned the awesome powers of their minds against him in an attempt to break him, to force him to return to them. Every step he had taken had been a battle against his own body, and when he had been forced to yield to the need for sleep, he had been compelled to bind himself to a tree or root so as not to turn back in his unconscious state and deliver himself up to them.

His head raised. Injured, hungry, exhausted, he had still made it. He had come too late, but he was here. He was free, and he had beaten their first attack.

He would stay free. Whether he managed by some miracle to return to his own time or was fated to remain in the Bronze Age, whether he lived for long years more or died relatively soon from want or violence, he would perish through an agency born of his own Earth. The Baldies would not have him and would not rule him.

Murdock glanced at the weapon he grasped in his right hand. It did not look like much to set against the crippling force of the aliens, only a burning brand pulled from his driftwood fire, but it would do the job—if he had the courage to use it.

They attacked again, determined to crush his inexplicable resistance, but Ross had braced himself against the agony exploding in his head. His mind remained his own. He could think, and he could control the muscles he must use.

His left hand was splayed on the broad surface of the boulder beside him. Deliberately, ruthlessly, he lowered the flaming head of the brand . . .

Ross sat up, stifling the cry that had shocked him awake. His heart was still racing from the horror of the dream, and it was several moments before he could completely grip himself.

Blast those Baldies! Blast every one of their thrice-accursed kind! He had no trouble facing the memory of that first clash of wills during his waking hours, but all too often, his sleeping mind seized on the terror and the pain.

Well, this time, it had been his own fault. If he had been spent after his morning's exertions, he should have refreshed himself with a swim instead of stretching out under this tree like some tourist on holiday back on Terra.

The Time Agent came to his feet and walked down the broad beach until he reached the edge of the sea. He breathed deeply, letting the clear air drive out the last clinging shadows of the unpleasant dream.

The scene before him was beautiful, but he studied it somberly, without any feeling of the pleasure it would have invoked under other circumstances.

Vivid blue sky merged at the horizon with endless blue ocean, which tapered to an exquisite turquoise here in the shallows. The water was warm, perfect for swimming with no even momentary shock of body heat meeting chill liquid upon entering it. The air, too, was perfect, hot but so freshened by the constant sea breezes that it never stifled or exhausted.

Everything was perfect on this Hawaika of the distant past. So damned perfect . . .

Ross Murdock pressed the scarred fingers of his left hand against his forehead, but then he took hold of himself. They were trapped, irrevocably, and here they must stay for the remainder of their lives. He had to accept that and do what he could to make the best of it, to make some sort of meaningful life for himself.

He could not! He could and would pull his weight, right enough, but there was nothing to hold him, absolutely nothing to which he could devote himself heart and mind, not since he and his comrades, human and dolphins, had joined forces with the local populace and driven off the interstellar invaders bent upon the annihilation of all this world's major life forms.

For an instant, fire stirred in his pale gray eyes. Ever since he had perforce become part of the Project and traveled back to the dim past on his native Terra, he had clashed with those ancient, deadly star-traveling people he had called the Baldies from their enlarged, hairless heads. They were the enemies of his nightmare and subjects fit for nightmare with their high-tech weapons, their fearsome powers of mental control, and their seemingly absolute disregard for life forms other than their own.

His head lifted. He had beaten them that time. He had been part of the team that had taken one of their starships and given it to Terra, that and a library of journey tapes which had opened for his own kind the stars and the planets circling them. He had helped to beat those same killers here.

The light left him again, and he sighed. Hawaika had been one of the worlds to which the Baldies' tapes had brought Terran explorers. They had found a lotus planet lacking any large life forms or history of life—until he, Gordon Ashe, Karara Trehern, and her dolphin companions, Tino-rau and Taua, had been drawn back into the planet's past, just at the time when the vicious earlier race was culminating their inexplicable plan to wipe the native life from existence. They had helped unite the peoples—for there were two distinct races—living here and had spearheaded the final attack that drove the invaders off. The loss of the gate through which they had come was proof of their ultimate success. Success and life for Hawaika, doom for him and his.

The young man drew a long, shuddering breath. With their gate gone, they were sealed back in time, in this alien world's history, forever severed from their own age, their own people, their own work. Three months had passed since that great battle. Three months, and already it felt like three years. Or thirty . . .

He scowled as a splash and laugh penetrated his reverie. A slender-bodied woman rose, leaped, out of the water some twenty yards out from him, followed in the next moment by two de-lighted silver-blue forms, rejoicing as only dolphins can in play.

Ross waved because some reaction was expected of him, but he quickly turned away and began walking toward a rock formation farther down the beach where he might sit and think at peace for a while.

The mission fate had set them had not proven a disaster for all of them, he amended his previous thoughts. The dolphins had adopted this time and world for their own, and Karara . . .

Murdock shivered despite the heat of the day. This world and time had quite literally been made hers.

In their battle to defeat the invaders, the human Terrans had joined, melded, with the three Foanna, the last remnant of the old, magical race who had once ruled Hawaika. Need had forced them to take that drastic step despite the danger that the effort might leave them somehow altered. He and his partner, Doctor Gordon Ashe, had come through whole. To be more precise, they had been rejected, cast off, by the Powers they had invoked. Not so Trehern. She had been judged and found worthy. Once again, he shuddered, and his eyes closed. When she had stepped forth again, she was something other than human.

Ross made himself watch the trio again. Her personality remained, or it still remained. For that, he blessed whatever gods ruled the realms of time and space. He had never been able to like the woman, although he respected her skill and courage. That did not matter. They were comrades, fellow Terrans, humans amidst fine but alien peoples . . .

Karara had been human. Now she was Foanna, or a shadow of the Foanna, and with every passing week, as she grew in the understanding and knowledge of the mysterious three, that difference seemed to increase within and about her.

At first, he had believed this accursed planet had changed Gordon as well, not physically or in nature, but in the relationship they had shared since their first mission together. He, too, had been able to deal easily with the Foanna, and he was a scientist, eager to learn and able to throw himself into the work of learning. It had seemed to him that without the Project to bind them, Ross Murdock had very little to offer to such a man.

The Time Agent's fingers tightened against the sun-warmed stone. He had little to offer Hawaika, either, now that her danger was over. He did not fit. His mind would not link with those of the Foanna, though they could read some part of his thoughts. Moreover, he did not want to give them greater access to his inner being and grudged even what they could take.

Murdock smiled sadly. In his selfishness and self-pity, he had misjudged Ashe's response to their exile. Gordon might be able to use his time better, but he was very nearly as unhappy as Ross was himself.

For starters, the man was an archeologist, not an anthropologist, and he had never been one of those lovers of pure theory who could sit back, joyfully pouring over the facts others had amassed as a miser did money he would never spend. He, too, had given himself to the Time Project and to the opening of the star worlds it had engendered. To be cut off from all that, to be forced into an observer's place, less than that, was as killing to him as it was to his more restless younger comrade.

As for the bond between them, he had been a proper ass about that. It had not broken or lessened, merely altered in the manner of its manifestation under the very different conditions under which they were now compelled to function.

That the archeologist spent a considerable amount of time with the Foanna was only to be expected given his education and interests and his good fortune in being able to communicate well with them. Lord of Time, Ross thought, unconsciously picking up Eveleen's phrase in the anguish and shame suddenly sweeping him, he should be on his knees in gratitude to them instead of nursing a jealousy even he recognized as childish. It was they who had finally succeeded in healing completely the terrible mental wound the older man had taken with the loss of Travis Fox and his colony. Ashe, unjustly, had held himself responsible for that, and the guilt, the pain of it, had very nearly destroyed him.

"Ross!"

He turned. "Gordon! Over here!"

The other joined him. Ashe was maybe a head taller than Murdock and was some years his senior, but his body was as lean and hard, and as browned now by exposure to Hawaika's sun, although he had insisted that both of them keep covered for the most part lest rays stronger than nature had meant their skin to bear prove deadly to them in the long run.

"Look at those three," Ross said, pointing to the woman and sea mammals with apparent pleasure, as if he had only been enjoying their antics. One thing for sure, he was not about to let himself be caught whimpering over a fate he could not change like some blasted spoiled adolescent.

"They've found their home," Gordon agreed, smiling.

He eyed his companion speculatively but then let his gaze wander along the beach to the tall-masted ship berthed at its farther end. "I watched you and Torgul today. It took you precisely two minutes and forty seconds to disarm him, and he's been training with a sword since the day he could first toddle. Even Eveleen would've been impressed."

A sharp stab of regret raked Ross at the mention of the Project's tough little expert in ancient weapons and unarmed combat. He had to make himself laugh. "She'd tell me fair enough and push me on to working with some other instrument of mayhem."

Still, he was pleased. It was Ashe who had insisted that he learn all he could from the people around them, particularly their combat and seafaring skills, as if he were preparing himself for another mission instead of merely warding off the deadly weight of time and trying to make himself a more salable commodity to better earn his keep . . .

He had obeyed willingly enough, although without real heart. It was interesting work, at least, and the effort did keep his responses keen and his mind sharp. It also effectively preserved his sanity. Between struggling to acquire the fine points of the Rovers' weapons of war and self-defense and the handling of the ships that were their lives, it was precious little time he had to squander as he had this last quarter hour.

Suddenly, guilt filled him, and he looked somberly at the archeologist. He owed this man so much. "I won't go back," he said abruptly, "not to what I was."

"I never imagined you would." Murdock had been well on the road to the life of a petty criminal when the Project had discovered him, some six Terran years previously, a boy with the instincts of a clan chieftain or commando in an age where such talent was a detriment to all but very specialized groups such as theirs. Ross had proven to be one of the best finds they had made, maybe the best. "You've grown up, my young friend." His eyes sparkled. "Except in the matter of patience."

"We'll need a lifetime of that," he responded quietly, suppressing the regret that threatened to flood his voice.

"I don't know about that," his partner told him. "If I were you, I'd plan on exhibiting my newfound abilities for Eveleen Riordan's approval a lot sooner than that. A matter of days might be a more realistic target."

2

MURDOCK FELT HIS chest, his stomach, tighten. He took a deep breath to steady himself, then met the other's blue eyes steadily. "Gordon, don't joke about that. I don't find it funny . . ."

Ashe laughed. "Calm down, Ross Murdock. You've been feeling rather sorry for yourself, I fear, to the detriment of your thinking."

"Go on." He would have liked to tell him in graphic detail where to put that remark, but it was accurate, and he was more interested in an answer right now than in verbally avenging the observation.

"Consider the matter from the Project's point of view. Five experienced, very expensive Time Agents suddenly vanish, and in their place, a full-fledged Hawaikan civilization complete with hitherto equally nonexistent flora and fauna quite literally appears on the scene. What do you imagine their response should be?"

"Put a gate up as fast as they could slap one together and get back to us." The hope withered in him. He did not dare let it run, not yet. "It's been three months, Gordon," he said simply.

"Our time. Besides, there would be the little matter of dealing with the locals and then locating not only the right period but the precise time, the month and week and maybe even the day within it."

Ross turned his gaze to the eternally tossing ocean. "Why didn't you say something before?"

He sighed. "Because I couldn't be sure. There were so many ifs, so many things I just didn't know, so many suppositions and out-and-out guesses. You could accept permanent exile, Ross, but maybe years or a life of uncertainty and waiting—I wasn't about to do that to you. I was having too much of a taste of it myself."

Murdock looked swiftly at him. "I'm sorry." His head lowered. "I haven't been much help."

Gordon smiled. "You've done your share."

"You said a matter of days?" the younger agent prompted, once more feeling the eagerness rising in him. Eagerness? He felt as if he were returning to life.

He nodded. "The Foanna shared my opinion and have been helping me watch for some kind of signal that a breakthrough might be imminent." He grimaced. "To put it more accurately, I've been trying to help them. The Lady Ynvalda discovered something yesterday morning, the beginning of a disturbance, that seems to be what we've been waiting to see."

"Maybe," Ross said sharply. The spacers had traveled through a Terran time gate once before, wreaking havoc at every level, and even all of their own race could not be classed as friends. Humankind was ever cursed by its divisions, and there were other efforts similar to the Project whose operators would use them as savagely as any shipload of Baldies bent on vengeance if they got half a chance.

"We're not going to be standing there with big smiles and open arms when—if—that gate opens, not until we're damn certain who's stepping through it and why."

Murdock's eyes suddenly went once more to the ocean. "Gordon, what about Karara? There's no going back for her. There can't be."

"She's an agent," the other said quietly.

"She was. She's Foanna now, or their creature. If she returns with us, the brain boys'll just grab her and take her apart, or try to do it. She'll never have any kind of life again."

Ross watched the happy trio, in pain himself at the thought of what they might so soon have to endure, worse in a great measure than his own recent misery. All three would be affected, too. Such was their bonding that what hurt the human would hurt the sea mammals as well. "Hawaika, this Hawaika, is Karara's place now. Let her stay, and the dolphins, too, if they're all willing. Just tell the brass they didn't make it through the fight."

You are generous, Younger Brother, and blessed. To be able to feel and feel for another's pain is no small gift, albeit not always an easy one for the bearer.

That sounded, not in his ears, but directly in his mind. Ross had grown accustomed to the Foanna's method of mental communication by then, but he had to school himself neither to start nor to frown openly as he turned to face the source of those thought-words.

The air before him was shimmering. In the next instant, it seemed to compress and resolved itself into a gray-cloaked figure, the Lady Ynvalda, he saw, when she permitted the deep cowl to draw back and the atmosphere to settle sufficiently for the Terrans to recognize her.

He felt annoyed and did not care if the newcomer detected his irritation. He disliked being perpetually taken by surprise in this manner, and he disliked these theatrics. He also failed to see the purpose of continuing with them, at least so far as the Time Agents were concerned. It was different with the Rovers and Wreckers, he conceded readily, but he and Gordon did not have to be kept impressed.

"Welcome, Lady," Ashe said, as was his right as the humans' leader. "You heard our discussion?"

"In part," she answered in the lilting cadences of her kind's verbal speech.

Ynvalda turned to Murdock. He could feel a shadow of amusement, provoked by his annoyance, but her voice and what he could read of her expression were serious when she spoke. "You need have no fear for our sister," she assured him. "She can protect herself and will pass through none of your people's gates."

"Unless she chooses to do so," he responded quietly.

The Foanna measured him for a moment. "You are right,

Younger Brother," she said softly. "That decision is hers alone. I accept the rebuke."

Ashe released the breath he had been holding. More and more frequently, Ross rose above himself, most often when the rights of others were involved. "I'll speak with her when she comes ashore," he promised, "though I think we can all be fairly sure of her answer, and that of the dolphins as well."

Gordon's eyes narrowed even as he fought to control the hope surging within him. "You have some news for us, Lady?" It required a surprisingly strong effort of will to hold his voice steady when he asked that. The thought of home, of Terra, was an ache filling all his being . . .

She slowly inclined her head in assent. "I do. The gate has formed and should open shortly, but whether it will be to admit friends or foes, that no mortal on this side of it can know or deduce."

3

ROSS MURDOCK CROUCHED low behind a tall, broken stone column, his heart slamming in his breast. He licked his lips with a tongue nearly as dry and clutched his weapon more tightly still with hands that already ached with the pressure of his grip.

If the Baldies came through, they would have a fraction-second only to beat them back, throw them off balance until the Foanna could bring their stronger powers to bear. Human enemies could pose an even greater problem . . .

The grid formed. It was the well-remembered pattern and proclaimed that the equipment being used to generate it, at least, had originated with their own people.

A single, slender figure took form. The newcomer was small and seemed shorter still as he crouched down, trying to minimize the target he presented to anyone waiting to cut him down.

The target she presented. Ross's lips parted in a surprise that would have been ludicrous had anyone removed their eyes from the gate to notice him. Although she was technically an agent, this was one of the last people he would have expected to walk out of the future to collect them.

The woman steeled herself and straightened. "Doctor Ashe, Murdock, Trehern, in the name of whatever, don't shoot me," she said with only the barest undertone of uncertainty to betray the fact that she was not perfectly at ease.

"All right, Miss Riordan," Gordon called out, "come on through. . . . Who else is with you?"

"No one. I'm it."

Eveleen looked about her and caught sight of the younger agent at once. "Ross Murdock!" She held out her hand to him. "I am glad to see you again. Both of you," she added, "but I never had the privilege of teaching you, Doctor Ashe, and so I don't know you quite as well."

Ross pressed her hand warmly before releasing it. Right then, he thought she was about the loveliest sight he had ever beheld, or, rather, Eveleen Riordan and that glorious, functioning gate together were.

Not that the weapons instructor was not beautiful in her own right with great brown, heavily lashed eyes set in almost too delicately wrought features and crowned by light chestnut hair that set off perfectly her softly pale Celtic complexion. She was small and slight, beautifully formed, and she moved with the grace of a dancer. At this moment, though, it was all she represented and the fact that hers was a familiar face that drew him so powerfully, not any physical perfection.

Suddenly, the ease and open pleasure left the newcomer. She stiffened and whirled to face the three Foanna, her eyes flashing as if in preparation for war. "Pull back!" she snapped. "Get away from my mind, now, and keep away!"

"Hold on, Miss Riordan," Ashe intervened hastily. "These are the Foanna. They're our allies, our friends."

Ross straightened. He, for one, could fully appreciate the weapons expert's reaction to the on-worlders' peculiar form of interrogation. "Leave her alone!" He altered his tone quickly, although there had been more of plea than command in it. "Give her a few minutes, Great Ones. We do know her."

"Peace, Younger Brother. The Young Sister has our welcome."

Eveleen moved closer to Murdock. She faced the Foanna, endeavoring to hold the appearance of confidence despite her racing heart. "My apology, Great Ones," she said meekly, "but we humans regard our thoughts and feelings as our own. We cannot readily endure the invasion of our minds, whatever the purpose, the more particularly since we are not accustomed to the experience."

Ynlan smiled. "It is so with the Younger Brother as well. Be at ease. Your minds are alike in that we cannot penetrate their shields, although yours inflicts more pain in your refusal of us."

"Thank you for that understanding, Great One." The Terran woman looked around. "Where's Karara?"

"There was trouble here with the Baldies," Ashe told her quickly. "Unfortunately, Karara didn't make it."

Eveleen's smile reached her eyes. "She has a remarkably active ghost in that event."

Before he could question that remark, the Lady Yngram, the third of the Foanna, intervened. "You knew us and what to expect from us, Young Sister. How can that be?"

The Terran glanced mischievously at Gordon. "From records left by Karara, Lady. She gave a detailed account of all that occurred here plus information on what to expect when a full-blown Hawaikan civilization suddenly appeared where none had been before. She also left instructions for your people on how to conduct themselves with us. Terrans' record of our dealings with peoples of different cultures on our own world is abominable," she added bluntly.

Eveleen shrugged. "As I said before, we don't like anyone meddling with our minds. With the Baldies' known powers in that line, we'd been working on finding and training people to fight such assault or at least to hold their own against it. When we learned of your abilities as well, it was decided that I might be the best one to send back here. At least, I was the best available on short notice."

"It was a wise choice," the Lady Ynvalda assured her. "You are strong, Young Sister." She hesitated. "You only mention reading of the Foanna. Are we . . ."

The Time Agent shook her head. "No, Great One, unfortunately not, though your memory is highly honored. There is a fierce long age between this time and that future."

"Can you tell us when? Or how?"

The human nodded. "If you really want to know, Lady," she replied reluctantly.

The Foanna said nothing for a moment. "No. You are right, Young Sister. It is best that those who are set upon life's journey do not know the hour or manner of its culmination."

Eveleen turned her attention once more to Ashe. "You'll have to produce Karara, Doctor. There can't be any thought of our taking her back—it's four Foanna, not three, that Hawaika honors—but I must speak with her. She has to know precisely what she must record for us and for her adopted people."

"She won't be staying alone," Murdock informed her.

"Hardly. Hawaika's oceans of the future are filled with highly intelligent dolphins who communicate both orally and mentally with their land-dwelling placesharers. To take Tino-rau and Taua would be to doom that sentient race to nonexistence."

Ynvalda nodded. "It shall be as you will. Our sister will not gainsay you in this."

The Foanna turned to the two men. "Would you like to speak with your Young Sister alone?" she asked them.

"If you please, Lady," Ross answered before Ashe could reply. "Miss Riordan probably has news of our own people which we are eager to hear and maybe a new assignment for us as well."

"That is so, Great One," Eevleen confirmed. "There's nothing we need to conceal from you, and I'm at complete liberty to speak before you if you so wish, but little of what I have to say concerns Hawaika, past or future. You may enter my mind to determine if I'm talking the truth. I think I can lower my shields for you if I'm willing."

"No need, Eevleen," she replied, her accent making a song of the name. "You radiate truth. Neither we nor ours will suffer for our leaving ye at this time. —When ye are done here, we shall bring

Karara to you. Until then, farewell, and, again, welcome, Young Sister."

The Foanna drew together. A mist seemed to gather around them, concealing them from the Terrans' sight. When it cleared once more, they were gone.

4

MURDOCK WATCHED THEM go with his usual sense of relief, then turned to the Terran woman.

She gave him a wry smile. "Those three're even spookier than I'd imagined they'd be."

"They're all right. They're good to have on one's side in a fight, and they pay their dues when it comes to putting everything up for stakes when they must."

Ross was mildly surprised at himself for that defense, but already it seemed to him that Hawaika was history, his history. There was a future ahead of him again, and somehow he did not imagine it was going to be either simple or easy. It was not even worth dreaming that it might be safe. That was simply not part of a Time Agent's job.

His pale eyes fixed the newcomer. "All right, Eveleen. Spill it."

Gordon frowned. "What's wrong, Ross?"

"That's for her to say." He caught himself. "Sorry, Eveleen. I didn't mean to put you on the rack, but you are, or were, an instructor, not an active agent. Besides, they'd have to have a damn good reason for sending anyone except one of the brains with a big degree or one of the ranking brass on what should be a pick-up trip like this, however much they want to try out your mental resistance. To my way of thinking, that means trouble."

She sighed. "Trouble in spades," she agreed, "though not for Hawaika. I was given the job more because of my weapons skills than any unproven ability to withstand a mind takeover."

"Let's sit and make ourselves comfortable," the older man suggested. "This sounds like it'll take a while."

"It will, I'm afraid."

Eveleen Riordan looked from one to the other of them. "You five turned out to be a full deck of wild cards, altering history in a major sense. For Hawaika, the result couldn't have been better, but the ramifications of the change went farther, and a planet called Dominion of the Sun-Star Virgin has less reason to be grateful for your efforts.

"When we got there originally, we found a world of large cities and rich farms and a human population who themselves had a form of interstellar drive and who had colonized all seven of their system's planets plus several of those belonging to the stars nearest them. They also had developed transceiving equipment that makes communication between star systems as easy and clear as we get on the phone back home on Terra.

"Their drive's not as good as the Baldies'. It's much slower, and people who make the journey out of Virgin's system generally go only one way. That's what's held them back from pushing even farther. Of greater interest to us, though, is the fact that they actually do their own flying rather than depend on journey tapes. That we want to learn from them as soon as possible and are making it part of the trade deal we're setting up with them, or we were setting up, to be more precise."

Her face clouded. "Our settlers on Hawaika had a whole civilization appear out of nowhere. Those of us visiting Dominion of Virgin found themselves equally suddenly standing on a cinder."

Gordon's eyes closed. "Lord of Time," he whispered.

"Baldies?" Ross hissed.

She nodded curtly. "Apparently. They must've hit the place with everything they had. Not so much as a spore or cell of algae remained when they left."

The arms expert leaned forward. "They had it in for the planet anyway. According to Dominion's old history, the Baldies tried to stage an invasion, but it came some four hundred years later, and by then the locals were able to see to their own defense."

"How?" Murdock asked.

"A form of mental attack that left the entire assault force utterly mindless. It wasn't pretty, apparently, but it was merited."

"How did our work on Hawaika change that?" Ashe asked.

"We've only got our probability and possibility scenarios to go on, but we think the ship you drove from Hawaika reported that her company had been whipped by definitely off-world humans before she disappeared entirely. Either Dominion was discovered shortly thereafter and was immediately blasted as a precaution, or else they decided to give her destruction greater priority than it had formerly enjoyed. They hit her harder and somewhat sooner in her new history."

"You keep mentioning the locals as being human. Are they, were they, so much like us?"

"That's part of the tragedy as far as we're concerned. They could actually *be* us."

"Terrans?" he asked incredulously.

"Possibly. Way back in their history, but well within the scientific era, the Dominionites had discovered some sort of time capsule indicating that their far ancestors had been transplanted there from another planet.

"Given the admittedly incomplete information supplied to us, we think another race, definitely not our Baldy acquaintances, reached Terra just at the time homo sapiens was starting to spread widely and lifted a few tribes, brought them to Dominion, and then artificially advanced their civilization before vanishing themselves. Possibly, they fell victim to the Baldies.

"Anyway, Dominion was already using iron and its population was beginning to unite in small towns and states while we were still in the Bronze Age."

"And they hadn't gotten any farther with star flight than you say?" Murdock demanded.

She looked at him. "They developed it, friend. No one handed them a working ship to copy. Besides, they had other things to occupy them. They didn't pull straight along a high-tech line the way we have, for one thing. They moved on the mental and spiritual fronts as well, and they concentrated a long while on developing and working with the planets of their own solar system, which they managed to fully utilize without raping. Also, they followed a considerably more pacific history than ours starting shortly after what they had instead of a proper feudal period. Advances didn't come nearly as quickly without the immediacy of major wars to drive them."

"Hold up," Ashe interjected. "You said they developed their own interstellar drive. Why didn't they just take the Baldies' ideas the way we did? They had a whole fleet of ships to our one."

"They weren't technologically advanced enough to appreciate, much less make use of, that bounty. They just destroyed what they took. Their scientists have cursed that folly ever since, but it enabled them to go their own way, including freeing themselves from slavery to the tapes."

Ross looked at them both impatiently. "Be that as it might, are we supposed to somehow chase off an entire Baldy murder fleet?"

"No, that we are not. The Dominionites have to wage and win that fight entirely on their own. Under no circumstances whatsoever are we to reveal our presence as aliens, not to the invaders and not even to the locals."

"Why?" Something in the way she said that, in the way she looked as she said it, sent the chill of his own grave through his spirit.

"The Baldies know there are humans, albeit primitive humans, on Terra. We've survived the return of Hawaika and the destruction of Dominion untouched, probably because neither was our own history. That might not prove to be the case if they took it into those oversized heads of theirs to play it safe and serve us the way they did Dominion, which they well might do if they found themselves thwarted by off-world humans yet again."

"We have to let her die, then?" Murdock asked sullenly.

Suddenly his head raised in anger. "We're not expected to go back and undo everything, kill Hawaika?"

"No!" She gripped herself. It had been a savage question, but it was a logical one. "We're not planning to leave Dominion to her fate, either."

"We've worked out a way to prevent that?" Ashe demanded tightly. It was more statement than inquiry. If the brass had not, it would have been pointless to carry this discussion so far, or to mention the disaster at all, at least at this time.

"We have, or at least the possibility of a solution. A lot depends on chance." The woman leaned forward, more deadly serious than she had been even while describing Dominion of Virgin's death. "Everything hinges on the native populace's developing their mental weapon in time to beat off the Baldies' assault. They had it in their old history. This time they did not. Something blocked its development."

Ross's eyes narrowed. "We're going to rewrite their history yet again, remove that block?"

"We're going to try damn hard. You wild cards did it for Hawaika. Now we're about to attempt to give Dominion similar service.

"We've found what looks like the crux point in a minor local war that took place seven hundred ten years ago, our present time. If the outcome of that can be altered properly, we should be able to leave the rest to the Dominionites."

Eveleen drew two maps from the wide document pouch on her belt. The first showed eight large bodies of land set in six expanses of water, all of which were peppered as well with nigh unto innumerable islands.

She pointed to one of the latter lying about two hundred fifty miles off the northwestern coast of the largest continent. "Not much to look at, is it? A little lump of real estate like that, and the entire life of the planet hangs on the outcome of an ancient struggle for control of it."

She lay the second map on top of the first, this one a detailed study of the disputed isle. "Here's our battleground."

"Glacier country," Gordon observed. The pattern of highlands and valleys would have made that almost a certainty on Terra, and the discoveries already made among the stars indicated that natural forces were at least similar on planets of the same basic type.

"Yes, by the look of it. You can see from the legend that altitudes are somewhat higher on the average than in such ranges at home, but it's beautiful country.

"The northern quarter's considerably rougher than the rest. The mountains are taller and wilder with narrow, rocky valleys separating them. The soil's reasonably good, though there's not a great deal of it, and water's plentiful, as it is throughout the whole island. The south has fewer really steep heights, and the valleys are broad and extremely fertile."

"That horizontal range seems to sever the two sections, the north and the south," Ross observed.

"Actually, the individual components of it are part of separate vertical ranges, but the effect is the same. For a preflight people, they form a nearly impenetrable barrier. Individual walkers or riders can get through in a few places, but only at this one pass here can vehicles cross at all or people in large numbers with any kind of speed, and that's closed for several months during the height of the winter."

"What about this war?"

"It's the same old story," she said with a disgust she did not bother to conceal. "It was a nice, balanced, feudal society until the ruler of one of the domains into which the island was divided got greedy. Condor Hall was the largest and best domain in the north, but its Ton, Zanthor I Yoroc, wanted more. Early one spring, without any warning whatsoever, he struck one after the other of his neighbors, swallowing them up before they could raise any defense at all.

"Only one landowner, Luroc I Loran of Sapphirehold, had time enough to give battle. This domain was the very southernmost, right on the barrier range. It was large, rich for the region, and well peopled, so he had a good army, or militia, at his disposal, but Zanthor had taken the probability that he would be prepared into consideration in his planning. Condor Hall possessed a fine coast and harbor, and the invader had made use of them to secretly import a vast horde of mercenaries from the Mainland. He sprung them on Luroc just as the two armies met. The slaughter of the defenders was complete, and backed by the supplies he seized at Sapphirehold, Zanthor rushed his forces through the pass to crush the forming confederation of the southern domains before it could raise an effective defense against him. In another two weeks, winter would have closed the Corridor, and he would have been blocked, but he had won the gamble. The island was his.

"His empire only outlived him by a few years. None of his sons or the mercenary commanders he'd rewarded with land had the strength to keep his gains. They weakened themselves with plotting and battling until the local people were able to rise and throw the lot of them into the sea and restore the old order as best they could, but by then, the damage was done.

"The mutation that was to give the Dominionites of the future their mental powers originated on the island. The seeds of it were already present at the time, but the enormous slaughter and the subsequent diluting of the remaining gene pool as a result of the decades-long presence of Mainland mercenaries put its development back by centuries."

"Wouldn't all this have happened originally as well?" Ashe asked.

"We don't know. We had no reason to delve into Dominion's ancient history apart from that one Baldy encounter. All we know is it's crucial to change the outcome of that war now."

She looked from one to the other of them. "Dominion was a lovely, rich planet, and her people were a fine, talented race. We want to save them, especially if we were indirectly responsible for their eradication."

"There's also the matter of their independent interstellar flight," Murdock interjected dryly.

"Yes, there is," Eveleen responded coolly.

"So we've got to delay this Zanthor's invasion of the south in some manner, buy the rulers down there the winter so they can organize sufficiently to meet his mercenaries?"

"Precisely."

"No chance of just blowing up the pass and keeping him penned, I suppose?"

"None. We can't risk Terra."

"Is the danger to us really so great?" Ross asked, frowning.

"Apparently, it is, given the sketchy data we have."

"That doesn't matter," Gordon interjected impatiently. "Great or small, no one's going to chance it."

"No," the other man agreed. "I wouldn't, either."

Murdock studied the map intently for several long moments. "What kind of weapons do they use? Old-time stuff, I imagine, since you're involved, Eveleen."

"Old time," she agreed. "Swords, bows. The basics. There are some differences in design and style of use, of course, but you'll pick it all up fast." She gave him a wicked grin. "They ride oversized deer. You lads'll have real fun learning to manage those."

"I'll bet," he responded but immediately returned to his perusal of the map. "Why a battle at all? Those fools of Sapphireholders have a partisan's paradise if those highlands are anything like our old wild country at home. Move everything of value and everyone into the hills where the invaders can't get at them and use hit and run guerrilla tactics against Zanthor. They mightn't be able to whip him, but they'd hold him the two weeks simply by removing or destroying the supplies he'd hoped to take, they'd stay intact themselves, and when the campaign opened up in the spring, they could rip the guts out of his efforts to keep his troops supplied. —He'll have to do that through the pass?"

She nodded. "He will."

"We'll have to start early. Homes'll have to be built and crops planted in the highlands. It's all got to be ready when the time comes so we can burn everything that's not portable and run . . ."

The Time Agent stopped. He looked at Ashe in confusion. "Sorry. I shouldn't have . . ."

"Go on," the other told him. "You appear to be doing just fine."

Ross's eyes returned to the map, although they did not focus on it. "We'll need the full cooperation of everyone, especially the ruler's, the more particularly if we're going to work with the necessary speed and secrecy. I'm afraid we might have a problem with that since no one's come up with the idea already."

"Warfare's a matter of open, old-fashioned slash and bash, not hiding in the hills," she affirmed. "I believe we'll be able to convince Luroc of his danger easily enough, but it'll take maneuvering and a lot of tact if you're going to manage the domain's defense the way you want. Even at that, you may have to make do with a very partial victory." Eveleen sighed. "That's why there's so much uncertainty about our ability to save Dominion."

The man glanced up sharply. "I'll have to make do?"

Ashe's eyes met the newcomer's, then flickered to his partner. "You'll be in charge of that phase of the mission," he told him. "You've already taken charge of it."

"It fits with our cover," Eveleen agreed quickly, before Ross could protest. "You and I're to pose as mercenary officers escorting our learned companion here. Doctor Ashe is to bear the warning to Luroc. After that, it would only be logical for us to handle the planning and conducting of Sapphirehold's war, assuming we can convince him to follow our advice."

"You?" Murdock asked sharply. "Will that be-acceptable, Eveleen?" He braced himself, although it had hardly been an unreasonable question.

The woman's nod told her acknowledgment of that fact. "Yes, indeed," she responded cheerfully. "Dominion isn't Terra. The Great Mother was never supplanted there—her people worshiped a nice, highly sophisticated version of Her right until the moment their civilization vanished—and women retained a position of respect throughout her history. True, there were no female Tons at the time we're discussing, but, then, there were no male priests, either. Just about every other profession was open to both genders, including that of mercenary. I'll be regarded as somewhat unusual since not many of my sex did take up that work but certainly not a freak, and my presence in that capacity won't cause any offense."

The brown eyes held his. "It's important for me to take that role, Ross, and to involve the domain's women as heavily as possible in what's to come. The mutation rose first in the females, and it's only through them that their race's mental abilities can be used for any purpose save straight one-to-one communication. The men will have to be able to channel their power through the women to bring down the Baldies, and there'll have to be complete trust and acceptance between the two sexes to accomplish that. It's as important for us to do what we can to foster an early flowering of that as it is to help thwart Zanthor I Yoroc's aim."

"My role?" Gordon asked.

"That of a wealthy, very learned physician from the central Mainland who initially journeyed north to study manuscripts kept in the region's temples in order to compare their contents with those in his own area. Three mercenaries, especially soldiers of rank, on the loose on that island would be highly suspect at the time when we plan to arrive. However, two of us could reasonably be traveling as escorts to a distinguished individual. . . . You have to be a doctor," she added, forestalling any question on that point. "Outside of the Tons or top mercenary leaders, medicine's the only profession open to a man that would give you the necessary prestige to gain the audiences you need.

"The story is that we two fighters noted the presence of a lot of our own kind in the port town where you were studying and remarked upon the fact considering the total absence of fighting in the area to account for their being there at all, much less in number. By dint of careful digging by all three of us, you copped onto

Zanthor's plot and hastened to spread the alarm. That you would drop your own research to do so will be believed. Dominionite healers of that era were totally dedicated to their oath to preserve life, though they never hesitated to fight when they believed that to be necessary. Reinforcing that is the fact that Zanthor's treachery completely went against the custom of the times, which is how he was able to take everyone so completely by surprise. No one believed it could happen until it did. Anyone at all, but especially a man sworn to the defense of life, would be totally repelled and would be eager to do whatever he could to foil I Yoroc's empire building."

"I'll buy all that, Miss Riordan, but I'm still an archeologist, not an MD. The mission will be a fairly long-term one by the sound of it, and if I'm called upon to act professionally . . ."

"Given your detailed first aid training and better than basic grasp of the medical knowledge of our own time, you're a small infinity better prepared than any of your supposed Dominionite colleagues. They're all functioning at the medieval level, don't forget. Just to be sure, though, you'll be given a crash PA course before you go in."

"It takes two to three years of intensive study to qualify as a physician's assistant!"

"You won't need everything, and you already have a good bit of what you do require," the woman assured him. "You'll also be bringing a nice supply of real Terran medications in your luggage, all artfully disguised. . . . Never fear. You'll manage quite well if you ever do have to go into practice, Doctor."

"Wouldn't it be a whole lot simpler just to bill me as a foreign Ton on the loose from his lands for some reason?"

She shook her head. "Unfortunately not. They simply don't go far from their domains. Any cover we could concoct for you would have to be melodramatic to the point that it wouldn't sit right. Besides, a Ton with no particular interest in the island would be considerably less likely than a healer to take on a voyage and a long trek cross-country just to carry warning against Zanthor."

"A doctor might also reasonably have an eye to a nice reward at the end of it all?" Ross suggested.

"Some generous patronage wouldn't be unwelcome, naturally."

Gordon nodded, accepting the inevitable. "What precisely are these Tons?" he asked. "Lords? Petty kings? It could make a difference in the way we'll have to approach and handle them."

"Neither. The word has no equivalent in any Terran language I know. It translates as something like landlord, or as noble and exalted landlord, rather, but there's a strong measure of clan chieftain in it plus a good bit of chairman of the board and company president thrown in.

"The setup's different than it used to be with us. The domains are owned by the Tons, but they're operated by the whole populace for the direct benefit of each family as well as for the whole. The Tons rake off the major share of the profits, but everyone working to earn it gets to stick a hand into the pot."

Eveleen smiled. "You'll be learning all that shortly. We all start training as soon as we get back."

Ross winced inwardly. He had gone through the Project's deep penetration schooling once before, when he and Gordon Ashe had assumed the roles of traders in Terra's Bronze Age. That was just long enough ago for a thin mist of nostalgia to have begun spreading a soft veil over the experience, but he had a very nasty feeling that the warm glow of memory was about to vanish in grinding exhaustion as reality once more raised its ugly head with a vengeance. It had been bad enough learning how to play the part of a Beaker trader in his own world's past. Now he would not only have to fight, but to lead a guerrilla war, and he would have to hold the pose of a native son of Dominion of Virgin while he did it.

He silently laughed at himself. He had been aching to get back to his proper work, had he not? Now he had it once more, and there was nothing for it but to grit his teeth and go with it.

* * *

The Terran men stood beside the waiting gate. Soon now, they would leave this ancient Hawaika for its modern counterpart and the weeks of study and labor awaiting them there.

When they were ready, or as ready as it was possible to be, their true work would begin. They would take ship for the cinder that was Dominion of Virgin, enter a time gate there, and go back to the age in which that planet's fate was to be decided. A sub would bring them from the uninhabited island that was the terminus of their gate to the threatened isle, though a chopper would probably retrieve them at the conclusion of their mission, assuming any of them survived to require its services. They would all be exposed to the same degree of peril as any of the locals while they remained among them.

For now, though, the business of parting held them. They had bade farewell to the dolphins and to their comrades among the Rovers. Only the Foanna remained, and Karara, who was still closeted with Eveleen Riordan, discussing the history she was fated to write.

Ross had quickly taken his leave of the strange trio and had withdrawn again before his open pleasure in quitting this place and time should become apparent beyond the point of courtesy.

Ashe stayed with the on-worlders. His own feelings were somewhat mixed, and however glad he was to be resuming his proper life and place, his heart was heavy. Whatever he and his comrades had done for Hawaika herself, they had been unable to help the Foanna. When these three now with him died, their race would be extinct. There was no hope of averting that doom now, and no hope, either, for the vision that had flickered momentarily before him.

The shame and defeat of his failure filled him, and his head lowered. "I'm sorry," he said at last. "I wish we two, or even one of us, had proven acceptable to the Powers ruling your kind." Only Karara of all the Terrans had been taken, and she was another female . . .

"It was not to be, Gordoon," Ynvalda responded. "That we

must all accept. Doubtless, it is for the best. Our world is death, soul death, for the Younger Brother and would probably have proven so for you as well. A change in form and ability would not alter that, I think. Ye were made, mind and spirit, for other work and other lives."

"Perhaps, but we found true friends here, and there was much we might have learned and accomplished."

"Friendship is not forgotten. As for the rest, it may be that ye shall win, both of ye, what ye desire in other ways and other places. The stars are open to your seeking and the plains of time."

Her head turned slightly. "The Sisters return."

The two women entered the room even as she spoke. Eveleen, small and fair, was the brighter in his eyes despite the shimmering aura that seemed to sparkle around and within her companion.

Whatever had passed between them in their long conference, both were silent now, thoughtful, as they approached the place and moment of parting.

Trehern looked from one to the other of those who had been her comrades. They were the last link with her old species, with the world that had borne her and the life to which she once had given herself . . .

Her chin lifted and a smile that answered to the force of her will flickered on her lips. She glanced once more at the newcomer. "Eveleen, you've told me what needs to be recorded but not whether I managed to produce a good book out of it all."

"A runaway best-seller!" the other assured her. "Planetary when it came to us and now interstellar, history and legend in one delightful package."

Karara laughed and tossed her head. "Now I'm not afraid to begin! I've always detested those dreary tomes one is compelled to read in school practically at pistol point. I'd have hated to think I was the creator of yet another of them."

"No fear of it. This classic's read with pleasure."

The time was come. Gordon's heart twisted. Ross had been right in saying the dark-haired woman no longer had a life anywhere else. Even now, in this moment of eternal parting, there was a barrier between her and both Murdock and Riordan. The fact that she had been human, Terran, and was so no longer stood between them.

Mistress of power she might become, but Karara Trehern was also a woman, a girl, and soon now, she was to be severed utterly from her own time, her own world, her own species. It was not difficult to imagine and to empathize with the grief and fear that must be burning behind that brave mask.

"Karara," he whispered.

She came to him, and he folded her in his arms. Ashe kissed her tenderly on the forehead. "Learn well, Karara, but be happy, too."

Ross gripped himself. Was he human at all or even marginally deserving of the title, he who pretended to set such store by it?

He took his comrade in his arms as well as soon as his partner released her. His mouth met hers in a kiss that was strong and earthy. He wanted her to know that, whatever she had become, warmth, the right to give it and the power to receive it, remained to her.

She responded with passion, for she recognized that this part of life, too, was closing to her forever. It was good to be held thus this one final time.

At last, Karara drew back, smiling, although tears glistened in her eyes. She took her place beside those who were now her sisters while the three who were to go stepped into the gate, shimmered, and were gone from her sight and time.

5

SWEAT BEADED UNDER his dark hair. Zanthor I Yoroc removed his helmet and cradled it in the crook of his arm. The day was warm, and he often rode bareheaded. None of the four with him should guess that there was anything amiss.

His heavy brows came together. Amiss? There was nothing wrong. The burning tug inside him was unusual, but he could continue to resist its pull as he had for the past two days. He did not because he was curious as to its source and purpose, and only by answering it could he learn the reason behind it. The Ton of Condor Hall faced the challenges thrown at him, including those that might originate only in his own imagination.

His expression hardened. No. The call was genuine. It had a goal, an end, even if he did not know yet where or what it was. For that reason, because he could not name the purpose of the quest or what he would encounter at its conclusion, he had elected not to come alone. Three doughty swordsmen accompanied him and one of his sons as well.

He glanced briefly at the young man riding at his left. Frail of body, slight of stature, lacking in the fine coordination and speed of movement essential to make a superior warrior, Tarlroc I Zanthor would have been a disappointment to most men, but he had the sharpest wits of all Zanthor's sons, and discretion kept a tight rein on his tongue. He served well as his father's clerk, and he, with his good mind, might prove a greater asset on this strange journey than the muscles and blades of the others.

They had been traveling for nearly two hours, but none of I Yoroc's companions voiced either protest or curiosity. They knew better. Condor Hall's ruler tolerated no breach in discipline, no questioning of his orders, by those he commanded.

He himself evinced no uncertainty as to his course. He felt none. It was as if he were following a detailed map save that the directions lay within himself. If he veered from the path, the pressure within him increased until he returned to it.

The end came abruptly. All five men reined their springdeer at the edge of a clearing newly cut, or burned, rather, out of the brush and trees of the surrounding countryside. The scene which met their eyes was such that they stared like children of herdsmen entering a large Mainland town for the first time.

Nearest them were three structures formed like straw hives but fashioned of steel or some similarly colored metal. Two closely spaced pillars stood at the opposite end. It looked as if they had once been tall, but now they were bent and twisted and blackened as if by some incredibly hot fire.

All this was strange, inexplicable, but it was nothing to the five men—the five beings—who had apparently constructed the odd camp and who were now facing the newcomers in a manner that suggested they had been awaiting their arrival. All were very thin and short by the standards of the Dominionite men. Their complexions were a pasty cream white, their faces long. The skulls gave them a grotesque appearance, being greatly enlarged and utterly hairless. The eyes were deep black, hard and penetrating, unshielded by brow or lash. They were dressed alike in an iridescent blue uniform that seemed molded to their slender bodies. Strange-looking devices depended from the belts circling the narrow waists.

Zanthor recovered from his amazement. He glanced at his companions and saw with annoyance that the soldiers were still gaping at the strangers, looking slack-faced and stupid. His son seemed equally useless, but even as he watched, Tarlroc wrenched his head to one side, almost as if by an act of will, and fixed narrowed eyes on I Yoroc.

The Ton gave a mental shrug and turned his attention to the demon-men. Among the rulers and soldiers of his own people, one who issued the first challenge from a position of authority often gained the advantage in a debate. It could prove so with these hairless ones as well. Better to make the move before they did. "Who are you who camp on Condor Hall lands without leave?" he demanded coldly.

"That we shall discuss with the ruler of this domain."

A glance at his son showed that Tarlroc's attention was fixed on the strangers. The others stood like statues or dead men, showing no interest in either their commanders or those in the clearing. "I am the Ton."

"We have come to further your plans."

Tarlroc I Zanthor drew his sloping shoulders erect. "And your own as well, no doubt." His voice sounded as if it were wrenched from his throat, but he had the satisfaction of seeing, or feeling, the demons waver slightly as he spoke.

"Is this the Ton-heir speaking to guard his inheritance?" one of the five responded imperiously.

"I am a cadet son only," I Zanthor responded with a hauteur that parried the other's dismissal, "the third of four such, but I know how to conduct myself—and what the bearing must be of those who would sue my father's favor."

There was a moment's silence. "Let the Ton and his son enter our quarters so that we may speak in comfort," the original speaker invited.

Zanthor smiled coldly, without humor. Did they believe him a fool because he had chosen to answer the now-vanished summons in his head? "It is a pleasant day," he responded smoothly. "We shall not have many more of them before winter sets in. Have seats brought outside so that we can enjoy it while we confer."

This was done, low, backless stools whose webbed seats were made of some material the Dominionite ruler could not immediately identify. Each of the Condor Hall men accepted one, which they placed, seemingly without forethought, so that they could watch both the strangers and their own immobilized escort.

There was no point and perhaps some danger in further delay, and I Yoroc raised the issue at once. "You claim you are willing to assist me. In what way do you imagine I need help, yours or anyone else's?"

"We would see you ruler of all this island."

The Ton's sallow skin darkened in a flush, then he threw back his head and laughed. "Conquer the whole island with the garrison of a northern domain? You five may be madmen, but I assure you that my wits are sound. . . . Come, Tarlroc. We have wasted enough of our time."

"The garrison of your domain could seize another, then another and still another if you strike one after the other in quick succession. Give the rape of the first conquests to your soldiers to whet their appetites and build their morale, then use the rest to pay fighters-for-hire, whom you would import secretly. Your force would then be sufficiently large to crush each domain individually, and if you move rapidly enough, the island would be yours before any unified opposition could be organized to stop you."

Zanthor remained silent. He had been giving serious thought to annexing the domain adjacent to his on the east. Swallow's Nest's Ton was old and in poor health, and the Ton-heir was of distant blood and little loved. That he could take and keep. What the blue-clad demon was describing was another matter, desirable, but not nearly so readily attainable as the other's bright forecast indicated.

He shook his head at last. "A handful of bought swords will not accomplish that. I would need columns, not mere companies, and I do not have the means to procure those. Commandants expect to be paid well, and they want a significant portion of their fee when they give their oath of service."

The demon inclined his head toward a large, square, white box which had been brought from the hive structure along with the stools. Two of his comrades wordlessly raised the lid and stepped aside.

The domain ruler's breath caught. Although the metal inside was formed into long rectangular bars instead of the familiar links, there was no mistaking its yellow color.

Zanthor's expression grew hard. "Why show me this? What precisely do you want from me?"

"We show what we are prepared to give. As a sign of good faith, you may take with you as much of this gold as your beasts can comfortably carry with the understanding that we expect three times its value returned to us upon the conclusion of your campaign. In order to secure further aid from us, you must deliver to us now good steel, copper, and other materials we shall detail upon receiving your agreement, and you shall give us the lives of your foes, their females and spawn as well as the men."

"You want us to herd half the population of the island here for slaughter?" the Ton-heir asked incredulously.

"Where they die or when is irrelevant. We only insist that they do die."

I Yoroc nodded to himself. That made sense. It would both punish opposition and reduce the likelihood of rebellion. The depopulated lands could be worked by docile settlers imported from the Mainland . . .

"Why?" he asked. "Why this hatred of them and your desire to help me?"

"We aid you because you can accomplish our will. Any more is not your concern."

"There are but five of you . . ."

"The remainder of your soldiers would be no more trouble to us than those who rode with you today. We would use them in the same manner. . . . You have our proposal. Do you accept it?"

"I have your proposal," the Ton of Condor Hall responded firmly. "I shall consider it in my own time. I am the one facing war. You are risking your gold, some of your gold. It is my life and my lands that I would be chancing. In the meantime, I will have the gold you promised to test to confirm that it is genuine."

"If you will have gold, we shall have payment. Your arms . . ."

I Yoroc's eyes narrowed. He shook his head. "Our arms and the arms of our escort, we keep. However, that carrion is of no further use to us. You want blood. Take the three of them as your payment. I shall come again soon if I decide that we have more to say to one another."

6

MURDOCK'S HEART WAS hammering wildly, although his will was strong enough to insure that his agitation did not become apparent to those around him.

This was not their first such meeting. His party had traveled the length of the island from its southernmost tip where they had landed, carrying warning of the danger overshadowing them to those Tons of each region whom their studies had named as leaders of the confederation whose success they were striving to promote.

They had met with a good measure of success, for their story was strong and the evidence they had brought to corroborate it had been expertly prepared. The various domains would see to their arms and supplies, and their rulers would meet to discuss the possibility of uniting to combat Zanthor I Yoroc should he prove the threat these strangers claimed. In so far, the timing of their organization had been advanced by crucial months, but no army would actually assemble, much less move north, not at this stage. Not one of the southern rulers could be that powerfully convinced of the reality of the hordes of mercenaries that would all too soon be marching against them.

Once again, Gordon Ashe had delivered his news and was facing the same battery of arguments, but this time, success, or the greatest possible success, was essential. They were sitting in Sapphirehold's great hall, and facing them was Ton Luroc I Loran and his chief military and civil staff. Fail here, and they had blown the whole.

"I do not hesitate to believe the darkness you impute to the Ton of Condor Hall, Healer O Ashean," Luroc said slowly, almost more to himself than to his guest. "I am not alone in thinking him no true son of Life's Queen, but that he represents such utter peril, that I cannot accept. Good though his domain might be in comparison with the rest here in the north, it still could not support so great a host of hired swords as you describe."

Ross felt the sour taste of defeat rise inside him. The meeting was going the way of all the others, and they would gain no more from it than the Ton's promise to stay on the alert himself and put his domain's garrison on the alert. That might be enough for the time being in the south, but here, they required a more concrete response. Without Luroc's full belief and support behind them, they could not begin to do what had to be done in order to preserve the domain as a fighting force and, through it, to preserve Dominion of Virgin.

Damn it to every version of hell he had ever heard described, what was the matter with these people? They had no trouble imagining that one of their kind could seriously consider annexing their lands by force of arms, but to a one, they could not bring themselves to believe that he could secure the means to carry his plans to fruition. By the time Zanthor taught them otherwise, it would be too late for everyone except the would-be conqueror himself.

His eyes burned in his impatience. "You're wrong, Ton," he said suddenly, breaking the silence that had fallen over the speakers. "Condor Hall can hire mercenaries and has hired them, and they'll stay long enough to fulfill its ruler's aim if we don't move at once to thwart him. It'll be too late to do that in even a few more weeks."

Murdock knew he had breached custom in addressing the Ton and the company assembled with him. Men and the few women who made a career of war for any purpose except to secure the safety of their native domains were not held in high regard, however quickly their talents were sought when reason dictated that they could be of good service. A mercenary did not inject his presence into a conference such as this unbidden, whatever his rank among his own kind. Eveleen and he would not even have been present had their testimony not been required.

The others there, including his own comrades, looked sharply at him, some in annoyance, all in surprise.

Ross set his hands on the table before him. He had begun. Now it was up to him to state his case well. He would have one chance, or part of a chance, and nothing more. "I'm a man of war, Ton I Loran, not a manager of lands," he went on quickly, while he still had the assembly's attention. "Columns, not mere companies, would serve Condor Hall for a short span, or longer if their troops were granted the rape of his first, easy conquests and their commanders promised rich domains in the south, to be held in loyalty to Zanthor, as part of their service contract. There's probably not one of us of any significant rank who doesn't occasionally dream of winning such a holding, however slight the chance of that's ever happening might be in fact. There're men in plenty who'll fight for its lure, assuming reasonable interim recompense as well."

The Ton's expression was dark as he studied the supposed warrior, but it was with concern rather than anger. "If that be so," he said at last, "what purpose was there in your coming to us? What can a few hundred soldiers accomplish against so many, or this joining of the southern domains, for that matter, if Zanthor I Yoroc can draw on virtually limitless hosts to support him?"

Ross Murdock smiled. "Not limitless, Ton. The column Commandants will serve long-term solely for the promise of land. There are only a finite number of domains, north or south, and Zanthor won't want to parcel so many of them out, away from his direct control, that he, in effect, would only be trading one set of rulers for another.

"No, you can't meet him in a straight fight. I don't think the whole north could even if there was time enough to ready yourselves. It's the Confederacy that has to beat him. Sapphirehold's business is to buy Ton I Carlroc time, and to preserve our own hides while we're doing it."

Luroc's heavy brows raised. "Preserve our hides?" he echoed.

The Time Agent shrugged. "It's my plan, Ton I Loran, the only one my companions and I believe has any chance of success. It requires a different kind of fighting, one that must involve all your people. If you're willing to give it a try, I offer my services to conduct it, or at least to prepare your folk for it."

The other said nothing for several long seconds. "What is your name, man of war?" he asked at the end of that time.

The Terran released the breath he had been holding, taking care not to betray the extent of his relief. In asking that he identify himself, the Dominionite ruler was giving him leave to enter into serious discussion on an equal's footing, thus permitting genuine give and take and open argument if necessary. "Rossin A Murdoc, Ton. A Captain of mercenaries."

"This plan of yours, Captain?"

Ross described the partisan war he envisioned and the preparations the domain would have to make for it to succeed.

He was greeted by dark scowls when he finished speaking. "You would have us cower in the hills like wardwolves, surrender our homes and fields without a struggle at all?" demanded a young man, very handsome by the flat-faced standard of his race. He was clad in the plain uniform of the domain's garrison, and a Lieutenant's stripe ran diagonally across his breast.

"I'd have you fight so you can win. It'll be a costly war no matter what you do. Conduct it as I describe, and you'll at least have a chance. You'll also more than treble your force, since all the able-bodied population can be trained to wage it.

"As for your dwellings and fields, you couldn't hold them anyway. Accept that they're gone until Zanthor's defeated, establish others in secret, and put the old ones to the torch when you must to deny Condor Hall's forces the use of them."

"That's easy enough for a landless, homeless man to say," the other snapped hotly.

"Easy or hard, I'm only stating fact. The loss is inevitable. It's up to you to decide whether it will work to your enemy's benefit or against him."

"Be still, Allran," Luroc commanded, silencing the reply the young officer would have made. "You offer to lead us, Captain A Murdoc. Are you capable of doing so? A man needs two sound hands to fight and at the same time control his mount."

The Time Agent started, for a moment at a loss as to the other's meaning. His eyes dropped to his hands then, where they lay clearly exposed on the table, to the left with its terrible ridging of scar tissue. Among people of this technical level, such burns would probably have taken the member itself, much less the use of it.

He lifted his arm so that all could see it and flexed his fingers several times. "It still works," he told the Ton.

Eveleen Riordan's head raised. "A man with the courage to hold his own hand in fire rather than give his enemies their will over him can also be expected to have the strength to work with that hand when Life's Queen so blessed him as to send him a healer capable of preserving it."

A good move, Gordon thought. It established Ross as a person of considerable fortitude, and it lay to rest before they ever arose any questions as to why a full Captain should bind himself for a significant stretch of time to the dull and relatively unprofitable business of riding escort to a wandering scholar. Gratitude for such a service, which must class as a near miracle, would be more compelling than any oath. Eveleen herself was posing as Murdock's chief officer, bound to remain with him whether he currently commanded the company to which his rank entitled him or not.

The frown did not leave I Loran's expression. "You ask a great deal on the weight of your party's word alone, Captain."

"Benefit only can come to you for following his suggestions," Ashe told him smoothly.

As he had anticipated, the other looked startled. "How so, Healer?"

"If our warning proves accurate, as we fear and know it must, you shall have preserved your people, your stock and crops, and your portable possessions. Not only will you have salvaged your fighters, but you'll have multiplied their number several times over, and you'll have so positioned them that they'll be able to make a major contribution to the defeat of your enemy."

"Truly spoken," the Dominionite man said dryly, "but if these mercenary hordes of which you speak fail to materialize, I shall have made myself a merry jest for half the domains on this island."

"On the contrary, Ton I Loran. You'll still profit well. Anyone who laughs will show himself to be the fool." The archeologist leaned back, clasping his hands before him. Ross half smiled, recognizing a glimmer of his old trader technique . . . "At the very least, you'll gain two harvests, and you'll have established fields and farms in the highlands, including the necessary dwellings and outbuildings. Should you want to continue using them, if only for pasturing your stock, it would be a relatively simple matter to move willing families up to take charge of them."

The blue eyes grew grave. "Less concrete but perhaps even more important, whether we're right or wrong, you'll have bound your folk to you with a loyalty that would send them through a wall of flame for your sake since you took such care to save them before the full scope of the danger threatening Sapphirehold was even definitely established."

Luroc nodded. His eyes fixed once more on Murdock. "You will teach my people, Sapphirehold's men, women, and children, how to fight this strange kind of war?"

The agent's mouth twisted as he suddenly recalled Terra's history and the countless generations of little ones whose lives had been blighted by her eternal conflicts. "The adults," he responded a bit sharply. "We'll leave the rest be."

It had not been a studied answer, but he could feel a change, a warming, in those around him. These were not men who sought war, even those who served in the domain's garrison. They wanted only to work at their various professions and protect their own, and it sat well with all of them that this strange fighter cared that their children, at least, should be shielded as much as possible from what he believed was soon to come.

"I'll show you the kind of fighting I mean. Lieutenant EA Riordan will handle the basic weapons instruction."

That last was met with looks of incredulity on every side. It was not so much her sex that sparked the reaction, he knew. . . . No one attained rank, or survived at all, as a mercenary without being well able to use the tools of the profession. . . . It was quite simply her size. Dominion's people were big. Every one of the men around them was tall and powerfully muscled in proportion, with a stocky, solid build that magnified the impression of great bulk. Gordon and he looked no more than adolescents among them. Eveleen Riordan seemed like a young girl barely on the threshold of physical womanhood. He could hardly even blame these strangers for doubting her abilities as they obviously did.

The weapons expert had come to the same conclusion. She smiled at Luroc. "I've taught arms use," she explained, "and so am the most logical choice to deal with the instruction of beginners. It's your farmers and artisans that I'll be teaching, after all. The warriors of your garrison already know how to manage a bow and sword and would have no interest in coming to me." She stopped, as if struck by a sudden thought. "Unless we have some different technique or manner of usage that they might like to learn. We come from a distance and may have skills unfamiliar here."

Murdock studied her speculatively. It had come to him that Eveleen fought most of her battles thus, with diplomacy, often accompanied by an air of not entirely manufactured shyness or even diffidence at times. It was a skill he had best acquire. Fast. One did not win friends and allies by stripping men, or women, either, of their pride and standing among their own.

He took up the argument once more. "Previous teaching experience aside, I specifically want Lieutenant EA Riordan to handle the weapons training. Your folk will be conscious of their lack of experience even after they achieve technical competence with their arms. They couldn't be otherwise knowing they'll have to go up against hardened mercenaries. Eveleeni's small and slight and stands as living testimony of what can be accomplished despite the lack of size and enormous strength. It's my hope that Sapphirehold's people will be able to carry that lesson over to their own case as well."

The agent leaned back in his chair, much as Gordon had done earlier. "It's a given that she's got the necessary skills, but you do have a right to see some proof of the fact. Let's go to your training yard and let her send a quiver of arrows into a target."

Allran A Aldar frowned. "You want her to shoot against my men?"

"No, only to show you that she can shoot."

Eveleen turned to the Sapphireholder. "What would be the purpose in a competition, Lieutenant?" she asked. "I have no reason to try to best your men, if I could, and I know those I'm supposed to teach are novices. Why should I want to make less of them? It certainly wouldn't do much toward building their confidence."

"Quite true," Luroc agreed. He came to his feet. "I think I am probably not alone in wanting to see something of what you can do." He ordered one of his guards to have a target prepared for the strange warrior's use. There was no need to command that a bow and arrows be given to her as well. These, she would have herself, all well familiar to her hand, and she would require or want no others.

Ashe fell into step beside Ross. "Is this necessary?" he inquired in a low voice.

"Yes."

Murdock turned his head slightly to conceal his smile. For once, he felt the older and considerably the more experienced of the two. Gordon was the fairest minded of men. He, Ross Murdock, could lay claim to no such virtue, and he remembered well the day that he and some of his fellow Time Agents had first been introduced to Eveleen Riordan. They had been a fine pack of thick-skulled young studs, and if they had known better than to openly voice either doubt or ridicule, none of them had been very friendly toward their new instructor in either mind or expression.

The weapons expert had appeared to be completely unaware of their hostility, but she had acknowledged that they had good reason to want to see something of what she could do before putting themselves in her hands, even as he had done just now with the Sapphirehold Ton. Since they were on the pistol range at the time, she offered to fire a clip after they were done, although modern arms were not her specialty.

The hand guns were not noted for great accuracy when fired from that distance, and each of the men's shots liberally peppered the face of their respective targets, most of them congregating gratifyingly near the centers. There had been knowing grins in plenty when the woman had checked her weapon and stepped forward to take her turn.

The sense of superiority had left Ross and his eyes had narrowed when she raised the gun, steadying it with both hands. She was not holding it vertically but horizontally.

She fired. The kick threw the heavy weapon to the side, then swung it back into place again for the next shot and for those following it until the full clip had been emptied.

No bullet-spotted surface presented itself to the observers' eyes, just one wide, black hole dead in the middle of the bull's-eye. Three of the bullets had gone in one atop the other in its precise center.

It seemed that Eveleen's father was an Army Sergeant, a career man with the old-fashioned idea that it was his duty to teach his children all he knew about his trade, his diminutive daughter as well as his strapping son.

Murdock shook his head. She had been right, too, in her own estimation of her abilities. Compared with what she could do with archaic weapons and in unarmed combat, her knowledge of high-tech implements of slaughter was nothing spectacular at all.

She had had no more trouble after that exhibition, certainly none once she began to prove herself as a superb teacher, but a lot of the men still held aloof from her personally, outside of the demands of cooperation put on them all by the Project. Ross was not one of those. He had soon come to like the slight woman, the more especially when he learned that her sometimes astonishing store of odd knowledge had been acquired through observation and private reading, even as his own had, and not from the classrooms of some fancy college . . .

They had reached the training yard. A good crowd was present, the Time Agent saw, more than had been at the conference. Word of the demonstration must have spread.

Eveleen was readying her bow. Murdock silently braced himself, hoping he had read these Sapphireholders rightly, that they would respond to the display of her prowess as had their fellow agents at home.

He also hoped that she would not somehow flub the test. There was a trick to managing these oddly bent bows, though in trained hands, they could achieve remarkable distance and accuracy. It had taken them all some time to master this weapon.

The first arrow flew and struck home. Another followed and another until he could have laughed aloud in his pride in his comrade's skill.

The last bolt stood quivering amidst the mass of its fellows. For a moment there was no response, then a loud, enthusiastic cheering broke from the onlookers.

Allran A Aldar approached her even as the woman stepped forward to retrieve her arrows. "Lieutenant EA Riordan?"

She turned quickly. "Yes, Lieutenant?"

"That trick you have of drawing and sighting in one motion . . ."

"You'd like to learn it?"

"I would," he averred, "and to have those under me learn it as well. I believe my father will want the whole garrison to master it."

Eveleen smiled broadly. "It will be my greatest pleasure to teach you."

7

ROSS MURDOCK STROKED his doe's neck. The tension inevitable to these final minutes of waiting rippled through deer as well as rider and was at least as difficult for her to bear as it was for him.

Lady Gay would not betray them, of course. She was as well broken to the demands of the war they waged as was the Time Agent himself. His pale eyes hardened. After a year of this life, they should all be accustomed to it.

Because his enemies were as yet relatively distant, he permitted his mind to range back to the morning when the long-awaited confrontation had at last come.

Sapphirehold's garrison had ridden forth in full pomp, supposedly to meet the Condor Hall forces coming against them as had all their neighbors defeated before them, save that their army was considerably larger and far better prepared than any of those others had been.

They had known they were riding into danger and had traveled warily, with hidden, well-trained scouts ranging the lands all around. Thus it was that when they had reached the place Zanthor I Yoroc had chosen for their destruction, they knew that hill-fringed field for a trap and knew what their course must be to both activate it and escape its jaws.

The defenders had seemed to rise to the bait of Condor Hall's own army ranged along the base of the long, low hill in front of them, but they did not engage fully, and when the erstwhile concealed mercenaries had suddenly crested the higher ground behind Zanthor's troops, the Sapphireholders had as abruptly drawn back once more and fled to the south in apparently total panic, their supposedly victorious enemies in full pursuit.

The chase had lasted a full two hours, more than sufficient time to permit the work back at the keep to be completed. All the while, the escaping party steadily shrank in number until the last warriors had vanished into the wild hills among which they were riding as suddenly and completely as if Hawaika's Foanna had teleported them to another world.

The Ton of Condor Hall had not bothered to order an immediate search for what he saw as a ragtag band of demoralized men who represented no conceivable further threat to him, and had wheeled his army about to ride for and claim Sapphirehold's hall and cultivated lands.

Smoking ruins and smoldering ash where pastures and crops had been were all that met his eyes when he reached the seat of Luroc I Loran's authority. The totality of that destruction, the utter ruthlessness of it, had frozen the heart in his breast, for he saw in it a shadow of the spirit firing those he had made his implacable foes.

That chill had passed in the next moment, but not the realization of the change this move would force in his plans. The loss of the supplies he had intended to take from Sapphirehold effectively ended his hope of pushing through to the south and crushing the domains there this season. It was late in the year, already past the time when a commander could expect to keep large numbers of troops in the field. He would not be able to supply his army through the Corridor during the long winter months and he could not gamble on being able to seize sufficient goods in the south quickly enough to meet his forces' needs.

It made no real difference to the outcome, he thought in the end with a mental shrug, apart from the annoyance of the delay and the regrettable necessity of feeding his hirelings throughout the winter. He would return in the spring to finish off any of the fugitives

who did not bleed to death or starve on their cliffs or put them to
the sword later if they fled south. In the meantime, he had accomplished his most immediate objective.

Zanthor I Yoroc had never been particularly interested in this
rough country the Sapphireholders called lowlands, not in itself,
but in winning it, he had secured control over the Corridor, the
single passage giving large-scale traffic access to the rich southern
domains. Nothing but time, the few months until spring, stood
between him and the possession of them now, or so he had
believed in his moment of triumph.

The Terran's lips curled into a cold smile. Zanthor had erred
seriously in his assessment of the defender's position. Sapphirehold
had not starved. Far from it. Both highland and lowland harvests
were in and had been bountiful, and people, animals, and crops
were well sheltered against the fierce mountain winter. They had
only to plan their vengeance and finish preparing themselves to
bring it to pass. Once they had settled themselves and had seen
the few injured out of danger, Murdock had resumed training his
army in this new kind of war, a style of battle so utilizing the
rugged countryside around them that it became a veritable ally
rather than merely a theater for their activities. Its value had
quickly become apparent, and the garrison's warriors had taken
readily to it, as did the rest of the domain's populace.

To the off-worlders' relief, Sapphirehold's women had responded to their people's great need and had entered service
beside their men. Most had soon established themselves as full
equals. Indeed, when it was finally joined, they carried their war
with a perfectly executed purpose and frigid fury that astonished
not only their own menfolk but the Terrans as well.

Full war command of the company was Murdock's. In the single
great tragedy of that day of foiled treachery, Luroc had taken an
arrow in the back and had fallen with brutal force from his leaping
buck. It was Ross who had dismounted and lifted the ruler's
battered, bleeding body across his own saddle and borne him out
of the battle.

The Ton had survived his wounds, but he was severely and permanently handicapped by them. Recognizing that he could lead no troops himself and acknowledging the debt he and his people owed this mercenary officer, he had formally given military control into his hands.

Zanthor had all too soon learned that he was dealing with no handful of pitiful living skeletons but a force of strong, able fighters who not only shielded their strongholds with deadly efficiency but so persecuted those of his troops venturing upon Sapphirehold land that the invaders dared do so only in large, well-armed units, and few even of those could hope to pass through the domain without serious loss to Firehand's ever more deadly followers.

Ross smiled again. He had quickly become known by that name both to his own comrades and to those upon whom they preyed. Murdock himself had been a little embarrassed at first, but Ashe had encouraged the notoriety from the start and, as usual, had proven right. It drew an aura of legend around him, a mystique encouraging to their supporters, disheartening to their foes. Zanthor I Yoroc depended upon his mercenaries, and anything that might unsettle them or lessen their contentment with him was to his enemies' advantage.

If the Ton of Condor Hall had been disappointed in his hope of utterly crushing the Sapphirehold fighters, he was more seriously blocked in his desire for the same quick conquest of the southland as he had achieved the previous year amongst his northern neighbors. The domains he now sought to annex had not prospered as they had through the stupidity of their rulers. Surprise had given him his early, easy victories, and the forewarned southerners had no illusions as to their own inviolability. Sapphirehold's seemingly suicidal burning of its resources and the winter that had followed so close upon it had given them precious time, and when the invaders came, they found a strong confederation waiting to receive them under the very able command of Ton Gurnion I Carlroc of Willowlands, the most powerful of all the domains upon which Zanthor's greed had fixed.

Late winter, spring, and summer had passed since the two armies had first met, long months filled with hardship and ever-escalating violence, as the forces of Condor Hall and the Confederacy opposing its advance grappled one with the other in the horror of total war.

Ton Luroc had concurred with the off-worlders and had not permitted Sapphirehold to join formally with the southerners as most of his people had initially wished to do. They were too few to make a significant contribution if they allowed themselves to be swallowed in that great union of armies. The domain's leaders judged that they could better serve the south's cause and their own by fighting a very different kind of war, that for which they had begun to prepare themselves before Condor Hall had ever made its first treacherous advances.

The land itself gave them their work and gave them, too, the opportunity to wreak real vengeance for all they had lost. Zanthor had not been able to strike at the southland without passing through the Sapphirehold lowlands and the single, narrow slit of the Corridor, and he was now forced to keep his army supplied through that same area.

It was a large region in itself, although small in relation to the total of Luroc's lands, too large to be even partially garrisoned with any real effect, and it was rugged. Above all, it was intimately known to I Loran's warriors and the whole of it was potentially within reach of the daring, fast-riding raiders operating out of the highlands.

The partisan leader made good use of every opportunity offered him, whether to strike the supply trains moving south to the embattled invaders or to slash at troop columns again and again until they were either forced to retreat to their northern lair or else to continue on to the front.

Even the Time Agents had not at first realized the extent of the importance their work would gain.

The two mighty forces had begun their bloody contest about equally matched in strength and in resources, but as time went on,

Zanthor I Yoroc found that maintaining his forces adequately was becoming an increasingly heavy strain, far more so than was the case among his opponents.

The southern domains were rich and well managed, and others not actively involved in the war gave freely to their support, fearing what was likely to follow if the Confederacy were to fail.

Condor Hall's empire did not enjoy the same solid base. The domain was a good one but could not begin to sustain its Ton's huge war effort by itself. The others he had conquered most assuredly could not. They had been raped in the first heady weeks of easy victory which had marked the opening of the war without regard to possible future difficulties, a wasting he now bitterly regretted but whose consequences he could not undo, not until peace gave him the time and resources to devote to their restoration.

With his own holdings producing a bare third of his needs, Zanthor was compelled to import the remainder. At first, it had come readily from distant neighbors fearful of sparking his wrath, but as victory in the south seemed to draw no nearer, help became scantier and more grudgingly offered, and he had to pay well to fill his army's wants.

Be that as it might, those needs had to be met and met promptly. He had bound his mercenaries to him through the liberal use of gold and the promise of rich southern holdings, but they were not willing to starve or freeze for his sake, not with their rewards as far from secured now as they had been the day they had given oath to him. The frequent, consistently effective raiding by the Sapphirehold forces was wearing enough on their morale without their falling into actual want because of it, and every wagon burned or stolen, every springdeer driven off to serve against them, had to be replaced quickly, whatever the difficulty or expense of doing so.

Thus far, I Yoroc had in the greater part succeeded in meeting that challenge, but there had been times when the mercenaries had been less than content, and each new success Firehand's people tore from them reduced their dependability as fighters and, more and more frequently, their very ability to fight as well.

Because of this unending pressure, Zanthor was forced to keep large numbers of men back from the front to ride patrol and to mount guard on the baggage trains or lose control of the area entirely, and he was beginning to sorely miss the service they should be giving against his primary foes, who were not slow in their turn to read his budding difficulties and press all the harder to exploit them.

Murdock straightened. Soon now.

He glanced at those on either side of him, Gordon on his left, Eveleen on the right. Allran, the Dominionite Lieutenant who was second in place to Eveleen and one of those who customarily rode with them, waited farther back, out of his immediate line of sight.

His thoughts snapped back to the present. Riders were just topping the low rise to the northeast.

His sharp eyes fixed on them. He counted quickly. Twenty-five, thirty, deermen riding guard on a dozen large pack animals. They were moving rapidly but cautiously as well, taking care not to skyline themselves any more than necessary, but the guerrillas had been expecting their coming and knew where to watch for them.

Ross glanced at Ashe, who caught his gaze and raised his hand in the old Terran gesture of victory. Their scout had not failed them. Their enemies would come directly to them; they would not have to so much as alter their present position to receive them.

The agent could feel the familiar surge of fear well up within him, but he kept face and body impassive as he raised his once-bright battle horn to his lips. It was a dull black now so that neither sun nor moon could reflect from it.

The invaders seemed to advance with agonizing slowness, as if they moved through water, although he knew they were actually riding at a good pace.

The thirty made a small column, but that gave it both a speed and an ease of concealment a larger unit would lack. Fortune had been with them in discovering it. They had missed many of its like since their foes had begun moving supplies thus.

Zanthor was anything but a stupid man. He had learned from his opponents' tactics and had soon realized that more supplies would get through in the long run if he utilized such compact trains as well as the more massive conveys which, although safe from destruction in the event of a single assault, were, by their very nature, slow and visible and subject to harassment along the whole of their route, however strong their guard upon setting out.

Murdock mounted, and the others followed suit. No noise escaped them, no sudden flash of motion that might have been spotted by those travelers still a little below them on the slope.

The partisan commander continued to carefully study the column, watching the way the individual riders sat their mounts.

He nodded after a few minutes, satisfied. They were wary but not extraordinarily so. They would not know of their danger until it was upon them.

The two units were fairly evenly matched in number, thirty of them, twenty-seven with him, but with surprise to aid him and barring some foul turn of chance, he was confident his party would be able to overpower and take most or all of their foes quickly, before the invaders could settle themselves into an extended battle costly to both sides.

The column had been steadily ascending and had at last reached the level of the waiting guerrillas.

The partisans remained motionless, scarcely breathing, until it was parallel to them, then Ross touched his lips to his horn.

Arrows rained upon the Condor Hall force before the low, soft note had finished sounding.

A few struck true, but most glanced harmlessly off the strong helms and the shields so borne as to face outward from the column's center.

It was usually thus on such a raid, and he felt no disappointment. His archers aimed high to minimize the danger of striking the valuable springdeer. Their purpose was rather to unsettle their victims before battle was joined than to fell any great number of them outright. In other circumstances, when different objectives were before them, his bowmen could wreak terrible damage and had done so many times during these last months.

Only that one volley was sent. The charge followed almost instantly upon it, well before the invading mercenaries could recover from their surprise to bring themselves and their animals into order.

They did attempt to defend themselves. They, too, had bows and brought them quickly to bear, but their aim was off, and they were given no opportunity to fire a second round.

The Time Agent felt a plucking at his right sleeve as he raced toward the column. He had no time even to glance down. The first of his foemen was before him.

There was no resisting the force of the Sapphireholders' charge. The skirmish was briskly, even savagely, fought for a few tense minutes, then it was over, leaving Murdock's warriors masters of the field.

Five of the enemy were dead, another eight wounded, one of them seriously. The majority of the rest were captives along with their mounts and baggage animals. The latter had been roped together for ease of handling and had, therefore, been unable to scatter during the battle. Four of the mercenaries had broken from the fray and had succeeded in making their escape.

The Sapphirehold party had suffered no damage save for a slight scrape across one fighter's hand and an equally insignificant injury to Allran's mount.

Because part of the column had won free, the partisans made no delay in quitting the battleground save that necessary to stanch the wound of the gravely hurt man.

They rode hard and fast for the next hour until Ross at last felt they had put enough distance between themselves and possible pursuers and permitted a halt.

His eyes glowed as he looked over the fruits of the raid. Twenty-six of the enemy were prisoners or casualties, bringing with them their equipment and mounts, not to mention a dozen fine dray deer. That were prize in plenty even discounting the bulging packs.

Those last proved a rich take. The unit had been assigned to the front and had been carrying with it everything necessary to support itself until it should be able to settle in and establish itself with the regular supply lines.

He watched with satisfaction the unloading of each animal. These goods would still reach the battle line, but they would enter into a very different service from that for which they had been intended.

Some of his comrades, Allran among them, were less pleased than their commander with what they found in the baggage. "Jerked meat and corn!" the Dominionite Lieutenant grumbled. "We used to eat better at Zanthor's expense."

His commander smiled. "So used his own soldiers. . . . Stop scowling, Comrade. Gurnion will make good use of this."

Eveleen overheard the exchange and joined them. "Pay no attention to him, Captain. He's just sulking over that cut Sundance took."

Ross glanced at the animal. "He's not much hurt, but take the Sergeant's doe. She's a good mount and should serve you well enough until he's fully healed again."

The other man nodded his thanks and moved to claim the gray.

There was nothing irregular in that. Sapphirehold was not part of the Confederacy, and what they took in their fighting was theirs by war right. Ton Gurnion was still surprised even after their months of informal alliance by the amount of materiel and the number of mounts sent to him by the hard-fighting partisan warriors, knowing no claim of his but only the generosity of these people and their perception of his needs moved them to give as they did of their spoil.

The weapons expert's expression was thoughtful, as was her voice when she spoke. "He's right, you know. There has been a change in the type of supplies Condor Hall is providing for its army."

He nodded. "In kind, but the quantity remains unaltered, and quality's still high. No warrior has cause to complain of this fare."

Ross felt her eyes on him as Eveleen searched him for sign of injury.

Her fingers darted out to separate the rent left in the material by the Condor Hall arrow. "A good shirt in need of mending," she commented dryly.

"Better that than the arm beneath it."

Both turned in response to a low whistle.

"Let's see what Gordon's found," the war captain suggested even as he began moving toward his partner.

Ashe had just opened the packs borne by the last of the baggage animals and had obviously discovered something totally unexpected.

His fellow Terrans joined him. He held one of the satchels open, and their eyes widened. Gold.

"The other pack holds the same?" Murdock asked after a moment.

"It does. Scant wonder the poor beast seemed to be lagging worse than the rest. There's enough here to pay off a small army."

"Probably its very purpose," Eveleen remarked. "Some of the mercenary companies must be getting restive."

"That's about the way I read it," Ross agreed. He grinned. "It seems they'll have to bear their discontent a bit longer thanks to our intervention."

Ashe's blue eyes sparkled. "This won't be going south with the rest, I presume?"

The other man made a show of pondering the question. "I think not. No, Ton Luroc deserves some little prize to gladden his heart now and then. —Do you believe this'll serve the purpose, Lieutenant EA Riordan?"

"Very nicely, Firehand," she replied, matching the mock gravity of his tone.

"You're in agreement, I presume, Doctor?"

Ross glanced sharply at his partner when Ashe did not respond. "Gordon?"

The archeologist's eyes seemed to be looking into the distance. His expression was puzzled. "Sorry, Ross," he said, recalling himself to his comrades, "but this is wrong."

"Taking the gold?" he asked in amazement.

"No. The fact that it's been made into bars."

"They're easier to transport that way," Eveleen protested. "The same weight in links would be incredibly bulky."

"Yes, and I wouldn't question it in our own time, but pretech and low-tech peoples generally don't abuse gold like this. They wear it or decorate with it or mint it into coins or some other convenient type of specie. Molding it into ugly blocks and stashing it away like so many spare bricks is usually the work of a more machine-oriented society."

"On Terra," Murdock said slowly after a moment. "Zanthor's ahead of his time in other ways, too, remember. That's how he managed to overrun most of the north and would have taken the whole damn island in short order if we hadn't come back to spoil his game. He'd probably be classed a genius if he'd turned his attention to some decent project."

"I suppose you're right," the other man agreed, although his eyes remained dark. He shrugged in the end. "I hope we manage to take Zanthor I Yoroc alive in the end. I want to have a long, close talk with that bastard, if only to add to the knowledge of our psycho people back home."

The partisan unit did not delay much longer there. The pack animals were reloaded, and the prisoners were bound to their mounts with their arms fastened to their sides, all save the heavily wounded warrior, who was placed in a litter slung between two of the springdeer. His injuries were indeed grave, but if he survived the journey south, he would receive good care there until he healed and then, in company with his comrades, better treatment than Confederates or Sapphireholders falling into Zanthor's power could ever hope to find.

Ross pressed them as much as possible without taxing the heavily burdened dray animals until they reached the base of the highlands, the point beyond which he would not suffer any outsider to come. Here, the party divided, most riding as guards with the captured column, the rest turning for their home base, bringing with them the gold and the animal carrying it plus the doe Allran had claimed and one other wardeer, a fine young buck that had captured Ross's interest.

8

THE DOMAIN RULER'S quarters were larger than any of the others in the camp and were marked by considerably more luxury. Furs covered a good part of the floor, and hangings of worked skins and cloth both decorated the walls and blocked the drafts which would otherwise have had free access to the rooms inside, a large public chamber and a smaller sleeping area. The furnishings, though sparse enough out of consideration for mobility, were of good quality, and several of the chairs were padded to provide for comfort as well as utility.

Luroc himself was still a fine-looking man of his race, tall and broad-shouldered, with heavy and flat but regular features and steady black eyes that seemed to read a man's very soul. His hair was a slightly lighter shade of auburn than was the norm among most of his people and was liberally peppered with gray.

Strength of mind and will were patently his, a strength nature had decreed should be matched in power of body. War had denied him that, however, and his legs now rendered him but poor service. He could walk no more than a few yards unaided, if his slow, painful shuffle could be so termed at all. To venture outside, he was forced to depend on the support of crutches or else take to a chair borne upon the shoulders of his warriors. Even to sit a springdeer was agony, but he could ride and did when strong enough necessity, such as the conference with the Confederate Tons and their commanders from which he had just returned, called him from the camp.

He was seated by the fire when Murdock entered, for the day was a brisk one for so early in the fall, and his inactivity rendered him sensitive to unaccustomed chill.

His dark eyes fixed on the newcomer, noting every detail of his appearance, so different from that of his own kind. He relaxed at once, finding no indication that anything had gone amiss on the partisan's recent raid, even as the preliminary report he had already received had indicated.

He returned the younger man's salute and motioned him into a seat near his own.

Ross obeyed at once, knowing the Ton did not like having to look up at those with whom he spoke, particularly if their discussion was to be of significant length.

Ordinarily, he would have launched at once into an account of his most recent mission, but he now studied Luroc closely, with no small concern. The journey south and the conference itself could not but have taken their toll. "You must be tired, Ton. I've got nothing to say that won't wait another day."

"What of your curiosity?"

A faint smile touched the other's lips. "I can stand it that long."

Ross started to rise, but the Sapphireholder's hand lifted. "Stay, Captain."

The black eyes pierced him suddenly. "Do you consider yourself disgraced before your own kind because of the sort of war you are waging for us?" I Loran asked him bluntly.

"With the success we're having? Not likely!"

The Dominionite smiled at his assurance. "Good, because Grunion has hired mercenaries, a huge column under Jeran A Murdoc."

The Terran thought quickly, reviewing the sea of background information he had studied in preparation for this mission. A blank shield would know by repute every column Commandant . . .

He remembered then and raised his brows. There was no larger or better force for hire on all the continent, or any other more expensive. "They can afford him," he remarked, "better than another year or two at war, at any rate."

Luroc eyed him curiously. "Any relationship there?"

"Somewhere way back, I suppose. . . . No, you'll find no greats or near greats among my kin," he responded with perfect honesty. The question had been reasonable considering the similarity in name and profession. It was this closeness in the sound of Terran and Dominionite names that allowed the Time Agents to retain so close an approximation of their own, as all preferred to do whenever possible. That reduced the chance of accidentally reverting to them in moments of stress or illness.

Murdock's expression darkened. "I bear my father's name and the name he gave me at my birth. If the Commandant has a problem with that . . ."

"Not at all," his host told him hastily. His voice gentled. "You are usually not so quick to take offense, my Friend."

"I was being a buck's tail," he apologized. "I'm sorry, Ton I Loran."

The other chuckled. "At least, you can admit it."

A flagon of wine stood on a small table near the Ton's hand. Luroc took it up and handed it to his companion along with one of the horn cups conveniently placed beside it. "Come, drink that to wet your throat and then give me your report. This proved a singularly profitable raid, and I would like to hear the details."

Murdock complied readily, concluding his account with his own speculations about the significance of all they had seen and taken.

"You talk of victory," I Loran said when he had finished. "Do you see it as coming?"

The Terran nodded. "Yes. I don't deal in hope and wishful thinking, especially not with you. I believe the crest has come in Condor Hall's war. Unless we fall under some ghastly cast of fortune or are guilty of an almost impossibly gross blunder ourselves, we'll conquer."

"You have not mentioned this before."

"No. It was the discovery of the gold that made me feel sure enough to speak about what had been only a thought. Token payments are frequently made to mercenaries during the course of

an exceptionally long campaign, but never anything on this scale."
He smiled grimly. "For one thing, the dangers inherent in trans-
porting large sums of specie are normally too great."

"Yet Zanthor did risk it."

He nodded. "To quiet his troops, I believe. He depends heavily
on hirelings and must keep those he now has with him. He knows
he won't be getting any more."

The older man frowned. "He has had no trouble thus far in
drawing columns to his standard."

"That will no longer be true. He'll continue to pick up companies, individuals, right enough, but he can't reward any additional
columns amply enough with gold or with land even in the event
of total victory, and that's been uncommonly slow in coming.
Those already with him will have secured full spoil-rights to
whatever domains he can expect to seize and can spare. The
peripheral profits which remain simply aren't sufficient to bind
potential newcomers to what still promises to be a long and
arduous campaign."

"By the same token, his current commanders and those with
them are beginning to tire and to grow impatient for their long-
deferred reward?"

"Even so, unless I'm reading it all wrong, which I very much
doubt. The cheaper, more basic foodstuffs and the alteration in the
frequency and the manner of their delivery give evidence of difficulties that weren't present at the outset of his assault, and, as
further evidence that he's in some trouble, many of our prisoners
seem more disgruntled than angry now."

He paused to refill his cup and to pour one for the Dominionite.
"All this is based on what I've observed in the Sapphirehold area.
Conditions could be enough different on the front to alter the
accuracy of my conclusions. What does Ton I Carlroc say?"

"He sees it as do you, although he is a trifle less optimistic. He
believes there is still a hard campaign before us."

"Hard and probably long," the agent agreed. "I said we'll conquer, not that we have done so. Condor Hall isn't going to lie down before us."

Luroc detailed what the Confederate commanders had told him of their plans and repeated their plea that Firehand's partisans continue their efforts, increasing them if possible.

The older man's eyes glowed as he relayed the latter request. "It appears that they regard Sapphirehold's contribution to the war as greater than even we had imagined."

Ross's head lifted a little. He was proud of his command's achievements, and it pleased him to know that the Confederate leaders respected them as well. "We'll keep the pressure on Zanthor," he promised. "As for increasing it, that depends on him. If he provides us with additional targets, we'll attack them. We have the capability of doing so."

"We can be fairly assured of ample prey these next couple or three months."

"Very likely," Murdock replied. "The Ton of Condor Hall has to have realized by now how little will get past both the snows and our people. With fall already on him, he'll have to move fast to send down all he can of warriors to replace those he'll lose in the final spurt of fighting and goods enough to maintain the whole lot during the winter halt. We should have excellent hunting right to the first blizzards."

"Your targets may be well guarded," he warned.

"No doubt. We'll still do well enough to multiply his troubles for all that."

The gray eyes sparkled as they swung toward the packs now resting on the floor not far from them. "Don't count on many more prizes like this last, though."

Ton Luroc chuckled. "I shall excuse you from producing that, Firehand."

"You'll have it removed to the village?"

"Yes, as soon as possible. We have other work here besides minding treasure. —How would you like to have your portion stored?"

The supposed mercenary shook his head. "Let it be. You have greater need of it. Sapphirehold must not only be free but prosperous as well. If you don't rebuild quickly, you may be seen as a potential prize by some other land-hungry would-be Ton. This'll go far in helping you to reestablish yourselves." I Loran studied him speculatively. "This is a small portion compared with what we will get once Condor Hall falls. Sapphirehold shall have full compensation then and an equal war share with the Confederate domains besides. That, too, was affirmed in our meeting."

"Treasure possessed is worth many times that held only in hope," he quoted the Dominionite proverb.

Luroc smiled. "You are a cautious man, Firehand, though I cannot fault a trait that has done us such good service."

He grew grave once more. "Understand this, Rossin, I will not see you ride from my domain poorer than when you came. Your swordbelt was well crusted with jewels then. It is plain now."

Murdock straightened, his eyes flashing. "That was a loan given in our mutual need . . ."

"And as such must be repaid."

"Not at the cost of risking again everything we've all fought so hard to save! When you can cover your contract with me and your debt without injury to yourselves, you'll do it. I'm not going to be a drain on you before then."

The Ton's eyes narrowed, but he raised his hands in surrender. "Peace, Warrior," he said with a trace of exasperation. "I consider myself a stubborn man, but in you, I have met my equal. . . . Very well. Since there is little opportunity to spend gold on these slopes, I yield to you for the moment."

Ross laughed softly, so that the other looked at him in surprise. "Peace indeed, Ton Luroc. We've been arguing as if we were sitting safely in Sapphirehold's reconstructed hall instead of still hiding out in the mountains. We may believe victory will be ours and be right in so believing, but we're a long way yet from achieving it. At this point in time, Zanthor I Yoroc has no intention of ceding any of his hoard or his ill-won lands to us. My portion will do little good until he does."

Now I Loran laughed as well. "I am glad no other was present to hear us just now! —Thank you for that, my Friend. Your work and my people's has often given me good news to savor, but a chance to laugh is a rare treasure."

He sobered once more. There might be the shade of a bright dawn glimmering on the future's horizon, but the present remained stark and hard, and its demands pressed sternly upon them. They would have to keep their attention fixed on the war that had become the central focus of their lives for the foreseeable time to come.

9

THE SUN WAS setting by the time Murdock quitted the Ton's quarters once more. There had been a great deal to discuss as they laid their plans for the coming weeks and for the following year's campaign should the conflict not be resolved before then.

Both were determined to strike again very quickly and to keep as much pressure as possible on the invaders throughout the weeks to come. The war would probably not end with this season, but if they could so disrupt Condor Hall activity that its army would be forced to take to the field for the spring campaign less than perfectly prepared, Zanthor might well then be on the full defensive, maybe battling entirely within his own borders, or have gone down in defeat before the arrival of another winter.

The evening chill was rising, but it felt good to him, and he resolved to remain outside a while rather than seek his cabin immediately.

He did not want company, and the Terran moved away from the campground into the trees beyond. He wanted to think a little after that strange interview.

Ross had said a great deal, too much, maybe. Mercenaries were one breed, whatever their world of origin. They did not make a habit of refusing gold or its equivalent, or of postponing getting a sizable hunk of it into their possession, either.

His pace slowed, and his eyes lowered to the already leaf-strewn ground. He had taken oath to Sapphirehold as part of the role he was playing, but he had realized in there as he had attempted to renounce his share of the war prize that he had meant that vow in fact. He cared deeply about this domain and its cause, not merely for its eventual effect upon Dominion of Virgin's history, but for its own sake and that of its fine, valiant people. He had not been able to bring himself to claim a resource he knew would be needed, maybe desperately needed, in the hard work of rebuilding that must follow the war.

A strange tightening tugged his chest and throat, and he increased his pace once more, instinctively hoping activity would dispel the unwelcome emotion gripping him.

The Time Agent continued walking for some minutes longer, slowing again as he gradually slid back into deep thought.

Suddenly, the sound of loud cheers brought him to a halt.

Ross realized he had been circling the camp rather than moving away from it and had nearly come upon the training field, the large natural meadow his comrades had set aside for working with their springdeer. He hurried toward it, curious to learn who was using it at this late hour and in what manner that such enthusiasm should be roused in what sounded like a good number of people.

He had his answer in another moment as he stepped from the surrounding forest to find the open place occupied by a sizable gathering of his partisans.

Allran and Eveleen were among them with the two wardeer they had taken in the raid. They were in the process of putting them through the series of tests which would determine whether they were suitable for the kind of service required by the hard-riding partisans or not.

That explained the crowd. If none of the raiding party exercised the right of first claiming, the buck would be given to one of the other Sapphirehold soldiers. The doe was already Allran's.

The latter had finished her course. The Lieutenant was standing beside her, surrounded by a number of the other warriors, and their mood could not be read as less than jubilant.

Murdock nodded appreciatively. She was a fine, clean-limbed

animal. He could well appreciate her beauty as well as her value as a war weapon, although something within him made him hunger to see a horse there in her place, a charger out of the past of his own kind.

The doe was not one of Terra's little white tails, of course, but she was close enough in physical type for Terran minds to view her as kindred with that species of the mother world. She had a deer's soft, large eyes and long ears and ran with a leaping gallop peculiar to those three-toed hooves, only the center of which came into play when she jumped or moved at her top pace. There were no horns, and her head and neck were graced with a ridge of short and very soft but amazingly strong hair. The tail was bovine in form, a long, thin whip tufted with a brush of coarse hair at the end.

His attention flickered to the second deer. The weapons expert had mounted him and was circling the hurdles, letting him see the lay of them before she took him across.

The attention of the others had swung to her as well, for she was about ready to begin.

Eveleen Riordan was worth watching when she sat a springdeer, her fellow Time Agent thought. Her ability ranged well beyond even the excellence that was the norm among their on-world allies, and she rode with a grace particular to her which made her seem one with her mount.

That last effect was heightened by the fact that she had set aside her saddle for the stirruped pad used in such testing, permitting her to feel the wardeer's every movement, to sense when he hastened and when he hesitated, to experience the rhythm of his gates, to detect any fault or flaw in him, to recognize where he excelled.

They took the first jump flawlessly, so flawlessly that those watching were stricken silent by the pair's perfection. Eveleen tossed her head in exultation. Her usually tightly bound hair was flowing free. She had apparently washed it since their return, for it wisped up under the teasing of the sharp breeze, forming a marvelous halo around her as she passed between her commander and the westering sun. He could see that she was flushed with excitement and pleasure.

Ross stood perfectly still. She was beautiful, he thought, more beautiful than any of those suddenly poor measurements by which the men of Terra set their standards of loveliness.

He shrugged then and laughed at himself. Ross Murdock waxing as eloquent as an earnest but not terribly able young poet?

He shook his head in half amused, half really annoyed dismay. What was the matter with him today? First, he had tried to refuse a battle-won fortune—albeit one he could not have expected to keep in any event—and now this sense of sudden revelation over his chief officer's beauty, which had been open for the seeing from the first time he had laid eyes on her.

Eveleen, ignorant of the reaction she had provoked, saw him and raised her hand in greeting.

Ross hastily composed himself and returned it but remained where he was, watching while she completed the intricate course.

The buck performed well, very well. He finished in exceptional time without mishap or refusal. Indeed, he seemed not troubled at all by his trial.

When Eveleen at last drew rein, Murdock began walking toward her. She saw him approach and, taking her leave of those gathered around her and her mount, hastened to meet him.

Her step was both light and quick, especially so with the joy of the ride still on her, and she had joined him before he had half crossed the big field.

Both paused to look upon the chestnut buck, who was now in a groom's care, before turning back in the direction of the camp.

"A fine deer," Ross commented. "He did remarkably well."

"Fine? He's no less than fabulous, a steed out of dream!"

"Take him."

Her head snapped toward him so that Murdock smiled. "Who's got better right?" he asked. "You fought well in winning him. Besides, you're perfect together. Everyone who saw you here has to confess that."

"I did want him," she admitted, "yet somehow I didn't think to place a claim."

"That hasn't been your habit. . . . Go on. You'll be using him to advance our mission."

The large eyes twinkled. "I accept him most gladly, and since he's sort of Firehand's gift, I think I'll name him Spark."

She was mildly surprised when the anticipated scowl did not follow that announcement, but it faded from her consciousness even as it was born. Other matters filled her mind, and now that they were well within the wood, away from the others, she looked gravely up at him. "You were a long time with Luroc. You were discussing what he learned in the south?"

He nodded. "And our own surmises. It's the general consensus that we're no longer merely fighting to survive and that we'll be able to start thinking about putting our affairs to real rights again in the reasonable future."

"Only Sapphirehold's freedom and the overthrow of that tyrant will ever accomplish that," she told him fiercely.

Murdock looked at her in surprise. "I'm not arguing that. Neither is anyone else."

She sighed. "I know, Ross. It's just been such a long haul."

"Well, the end's coming, even if we do still have a damn hard fight ahead of us."

He detailed for her what had passed between I Loran and himself on the subject and then, speaking more slowly, outlined his plans—as yet only ideas—for sharpening their campaign against the invaders, clarifying his thoughts even as he spoke.

Eveleen questioned a few points, added to others, inserted ideas of her own which Ross, in turn, parried and tested. Time passed as their conversation became more and more intricately involved until both realized with a start that full night had fallen unnoticed while they had talked.

They had instinctively stopped at the edge of the camp, which was now outlined in the flickering light of the fires.

All the weariness of the past days seemed to settle over Murdock in that moment. He flexed his shoulders to ease the ache of which he had suddenly become aware. "I'll call the others to council tomorrow. For now, I think we'd both benefit from some sleep."

She offered no protest to that, and they walked quickly in the direction of their quarters, silent now, each busy with thoughts of the work before them.

After seeing his companion to her cabin, Murdock made no delay in seeking out the small building housing both his own sleeping chamber and his office.

There was light inside, dim, cast by a candle left standing on the table that served him as his desk.

This, he took up without glancing at any of the papers neatly piled there awaiting his attention and went directly to the inner room. He automatically touched the burning wick to that of the taper fastened to the wall by the door. The latter took fire, flickered, and then steadied.

The increased light, little though it was, seemed harsh to tired eyes accustomed to the night and unwilling to adapt swiftly to this change in illumination, and he pinched out the candle in his hand.

He set it down and gave a hurried glance around his quarters that yet missed no detail.

Everything was in order, better order than he should have found. He started to frown. His fighting gear was in its place, clean and ready for his use. He had not left it so.

Ross sat down on the narrow bed. That, too, had been made ready for him.

A soft knock sounded at the door, and even as he glanced up Gordon Ashe came into the room.

"You didn't have to do this," Murdock said dully.

"No, but I figured you'd be tied up with Luroc for half the evening and be dead tired afterward. A partisan should be able to sleep for a few hours following one of our raids, not have to hop right into a council of war."

He sighed. "Well, the favor's appreciated tonight. Thanks."

The guerrilla commander looked up suddenly. "I Loran offered me my share of the gold."

Ashe's brows raised, and his lips curved into an amused smile. "I suppose there'll eventually be some sort of ruling against it—conflict of interest or some such thing—but as of the moment, there's no law against . . ."

"Can it, will you, Gordon! I don't think that's funny." He gripped himself. "Sorry. I'm about done, I guess."

"You are." The other was deadly serious now. "You're also finding that you like Dominion of Virgin a great deal and that you could make it here, make it big."

A knife seemed to drive into Ross, and he turned away swiftly, his head lowering.

Ashe's fingers closed on his shoulder. "Karara stayed, Ross," he reminded him gently. "Only, think carefully, very, very carefully, before you choose this world and time to be your Hawaika."

10

G ET OUT!"
Zanthor's eyes bore into the back of the retreating mercenary until the door of his office closed between them. His fist slammed onto the surface of the table that was his desk. "Firehand again! May every demon's curse blight his life!"

"Demons' curses are readily summoned," Tarlroc I Zanthor replied calmly. "That was the last of their gold."

"The last of it in our possession," his sire corrected.

"You will go to them again so soon?"

"I need that gold," he responded bluntly. "Our hirelings had taken possession of their payment and lost it themselves, but I still must send them some sop to ease their disappointment, or I might find myself lacking an army come spring. How long do you think it would be after that before we were all spitted on I Carlroc's swords or on those of Firehand's skulkers in the shadows?"

"That could prove the lesser of our perils."

The tightness in his tone caused the older man to look at him sharply. "You fear the big heads so greatly?" he asked contemptuously.

"I fear them, and so should you." He hesitated. "You feel nothing when we are with them? They do nothing to you?"

I Yoroc started to snap out a curt denial but changed his mind. "Nothing, or nothing since they guided me to them the first time." He described the strange pulling he had experienced then.

"Maybe you are safe," Tarlroc said softly, more to himself than to his father. "That would explain . . ."

"I do not see that they have done you much harm."

"Not for lack of effort on their part," he responded bitterly. "They attempted to freeze me along with the rest of your escort, but I freed myself." He shivered in his heart. He was good with words, but he could not describe that horrible burning, the invisible fire that had threatened to sear away his mind, to char the core of his being. He could not explain how he had been able to block it. He simply did not know, save that it had cost an enormous effort of will to do so. "Even then, they did not leave me alone. They have never ceased trying to bend me to their will."

"In what manner?" Zanthor demanded. "You have not chosen to mention this before."

Tarlroc's eyes fell. "They press me to kill you."

"The demons ordered that?"

"Not directly, but thoughts rise in me when we are with them, memories of slights, insults, blows. Some of the incidents did happen, but the most of them have to be creations of the hairless ones. They do not come of me."

"Obviously, you have resisted. Thus far."

His son looked up. "I do not want to kill you," he said quietly. "You have used me well enough when another man might have looked at me and done otherwise. You have appreciated the abilities I do have and put them to good use, granting me even greater access to your councils than you do the Ton-heir . . ."

Tarlroc saw Zanthor's impatient scowl, and his head raised. "I am not growing maudlin or stupid, but we are treating with demons who can draw people to them, reduce soldiers to breathing corpses, insert thoughts and promptings into men's minds. We would do well to be clear about our own intentions and interests when we front them, or we could find ourselves serving theirs only."

"You have a head balanced on that scrawny neck," the Ton of Condor Hall conceded gruffly. "So they try to lure you into slaying me? Why? Why not do it themselves, for that matter?

Those fire rods they made sure we saw them use the last time could burn through flesh as readily as through steel."

"Who knows what moves their kind? They may feel they have a better hope of controlling me for their own ends. Whatever their reasons, they do seem to want us, you, to do their butchering for them, though I would not trust them far once we do gain control of the island." His mouth twisted. "If we do."

"We are not beaten yet," I Yoroc told him calmly. "As for trusting them, you may rest assured that I do not, in my sight or out of it. They are allies of need at this point, not of choice."

Zanthor's eyes were hard, determined. "Order our deer saddled. The big heads will not be expecting another visit from us at this point. Perhaps we can surprise some concessions out of them."

The Condor Hall leaders silently made their way along the familiar route. The Ton was deep in thought, as he had been almost from the time they had left the hall. His son welcomed the quiet as he strove to strengthen himself against the compulsion to which he knew he would be subjected.

Suddenly, I Yoroc reined in his mount. "I would prefer to give the demons as little notice of our approach as possible. Let us go the rest of the way on foot."

They fastened the springdeer to a tree near a good patch of browse. The route before them was in actuality a rough path worn by the strange beings in the camp, and they would be able to travel it quietly and quickly, with no snapping or swishing branches to announce their presence.

The Dominionites soon reached the clearing. Those they sought were there, deeply engrossed in heavy, well-ordered labor.

The two damaged pillars were lying on the ground, as they had been since the humans' second visit, and the five strangers were working on them. Already, they had straightened them. Splotches of somewhat differently colored metal revealed where patches had been added to strengthen the original structures and for other purposes incomprehensible to the two observers. A pair of the demons were using their fire rods to melt some of Zanthor's latest offering in preparation to melding it to the column on which they presently worked.

The watchers were given only a brief moment in which to study the camp. In the next, the hairless ones straightened and faced the place where they were standing.

I Yoroc called out his name and stepped forward, keeping his hands well away from his sword. Tarlroc followed a step behind him.

"Put up your fire rods. As always, we come in peace."

"This was poorly done, Ton. Why do you spy on us?"

"Taking a moment's breathing space is not spying," he countered evenly. "Why do you order my son to kill me?"

There was no immediate answer, and Zanthor's eyes narrowed. "Did you think he would not inform me of your efforts?"

"It was merely to test his loyalty as your close associate."

"Your caution is greatly appreciated," I Yoroc commented dryly, "but he has met the test. It need not be repeated."

"This is why you have returned here so soon?"

"I am here because I, in my turn, feel compelled to put your supposed goodwill to the test. I want the remainder of the gold now. I have a war to fight which I began at your instigation. Paltry doles will not win it for me or for you."

"You have not brought us a third of the material we requested," the demons' spokesman told him.

"I have brought you all I am going to bring until the Confederation is broken," the Ton of Condor Hall snapped. "I need steel for arms and armor. The rest is either difficult to procure or hard to produce when I require my craftsfolk for direct war work. When my enemies are dead, you shall receive our payment, not before."

It was impossible to read the hairless ones' expressions, but Zanthor knew they were displeased and maybe furious. If he had erred in his reasoning concerning them . . .

After several tense seconds, the demon nodded in the direction of the chest. "What is there, you may take. You will have no more from us, either gold or any active aid, until you have given us what you have pledged yourself to supply."

The Dominionites led their heavily laden deer. Only when they neared the hall would they mount in order to avoid drawing undue attention to themselves.

Tarlroc's face was white, and his fingers trembled as they clutched the reins. Such hatred. He shuddered to think what it would have done had it burned into him. Had they been trying that and failed or simply feeling their anger as he had felt his fear? He glanced enviously at his father. Zanthor had appeared to be oblivious to the invisible storm his refusal and arrogance had generated.

The young man moistened his lips. The storm would be neither silent nor invisible if I Yoroc caught him still shaking a full hour after the confrontation had ended. "How are you going to ensure that the next shipment reaches our troops?" he ventured.

Zanthor gave him a superior smile and slowed his pace so that they might walk companionably together. "By sending a little on one convoy, a little with another. The bulk of this will be reserved for other expenses and for our own troops. The mercenaries will have to make themselves content with that. I turned our contracted payment over to Commandant A Huron's representative at Condor Hall and have his receipt as proof. It was our hirelings' own property and was traveling in their own care when they lost it. I am not obligated to restore the full amount to them. The same is true of the supplies, but I shall, of course, replace those."

"How?"

"I'll send a few large shipments and a lot of small ones."

"Firehand . . ."

"He has hurt us badly and will continue to do so as we provide him with additional targets, but enough will get through. Our army will not fatten this winter, but it will not freeze or starve— though I want I Carlroc to believe otherwise."

His son drew a deep breath. "Do—do you believe there is still a real chance?"

Zanthor I Yoroc laughed. "With some luck and a lot of care, there will be victory. Let the war go on as it has until winter, with the Confederates believing we are nigh unto bled to death. Come spring, my mercenaries can renew the fight in full vigor."

"Renew the stalemate. At best, the stalemate," Tarlroc responded bitterly.

"Ah, yes, but I plan to assume direct command of the fighting myself and to release our own Condor Hall troops as well."

"Will that be sufficient to beat the Confederates back? They are strong . . ."

"We shall not even try. It is the Confederation we will attack, not its army. Luroc I Loran taught the lesson. Now we will show how well we have learned it.

"My troops will push right through the lines, slip through if we can, while our hirelings engage their army. Once behind them, we shall head south, putting to the sword every man, woman, and child that we find. Every animal we cannot drive off will be slaughtered. Everything we cannot carry will be burned. Let us see how long Gurnion I Carlroc's army holds together once the Tons learn their whelps' blood is soaking the ashes of their ruined halls and fields.

"We can eliminate them individually as we originally intended and then return to hunt out Firehand at our leisure."

"Then you will pay the demons?"

Zanthor pursed his lips. "Those hairless ones appear very eager to get the materials they have demanded. I wonder seriously what they will do once they lay their hands on it."

"They will do themselves what they have urged me to do," Tarlroc predicted darkly.

The Ton chuckled. "You worry a great deal, Tarlroc I Zanthor. Demons they may be, but they have proven unable to command or damage either of us with their tricks of mind." He slapped the hilt of his sword. "Steel, they shall have, right enough, but that comes in many forms. They will not enjoy the manner in which I intend to deliver it."

11

WHATEVER HIS EXHAUSTION and the confused, now un-remembered dreams that had troubled his sleep, Murdock awoke at his customary time the following morning.

He lay still a few minutes, enjoying the luxury of the bed and the warmth of his cabin after the rugged living of the past several days.

Ross brushed aside the blanket covering him and then paused to look at it. He had slipped off his boots and lain back without troubling to draw it over himself. Gordon must have done this, too, before he had finally left for his own quarters.

He shook his head. Sleep must have hit him with the force of a poleax for him to have remained oblivious to that.

Whatever about it, the night's rest had served him well. He was relaxed and refreshed and, he realized, enormously hungry.

The floor in front of him was striped with bands of gold, sunlight streaming in through the slats of the shutters covering the single unglazed window.

He arose and opened the shutters. The morning was beautiful, the sky was a vibrant blue, the air brisk and clear.

Ashe must have been watching for this sign, for he came to the cabin a few minutes later carrying with him both food and water for washing.

Murdock was not long in readying himself. He sat down to eat at the all-purpose desk table while his partner gave him an account of affairs in the camp, a surprisingly detailed one considering the fact that he, too, had only returned to it the previous afternoon. He had put the time Ross had spent with the Ton to good use.

The other man eyed his rapidly emptied plate with satisfaction, then turned his attention to Ross himself. "I'm glad to find you looking somewhat less like a casualty this morning."

"I feel less like one." He looked a bit sheepish. "I'm afraid I tried to snap the head off you last night."

Gordon smiled. "There aren't many people at whom a commander in a situation like ours can afford to snarl. He also can't afford to take on the man-of-iron pose. That goes down poorly with mere mortals."

Ross nodded ruefully. "I've been getting good practice walking the middle line on this job." Personally, he had long since come to the conclusion that being the junior partner in such a venture had its advantages.

His eyes darkened. "I worry sometimes, Gordon. You should be the one in charge. I'm fine in the field, but when it comes to planning the war, even just Sapphirehold's part in it, and planning what has to come afterward so these people can rebuild . . ."

"You're doing fine," the archeologist responded quietly. "As a learned scholar and one by now intimately involved in the domain's affairs, I probably will be drawn into some of the reconstruction discussions, but I can't see that I'll have to do more than back up your decisions and I Loran's. Sapphirehold's present and future affairs are in very competent hands."

Murdock smiled his thanks. "I hope you're right, my friend. It seems a lot to be hanging on the judgment of a former minor hood."

He shrugged then. "Is Eveleen up yet?"

"Yes, hard as it is to roust her out of her bed the day after a raid. I saw her just as I was bringing breakfast to you."

"I'd best go find her," Ross said more to himself than to the other. "We've got a lot to discuss."

"She should still be eating. There's no panic on for once."

* * *

Ross stood in the doorway until he spotted Eveleen sitting by herself on a grassy knoll near the first line of trees. The weapons expert liked to take her breakfast outside whenever the weather permitted, especially when things were quiet and no urgent duty pressed her.

He walked over to her, moving with a brisk, determined step that belied the general air of peace resting on the camp.

Murdock noted that her hair was up once more, but it was softly styled, like the Dominionite women used to wear theirs before war had driven them from their homes. Doubtless, she had her net near to hand, ready to snap into place should danger threaten or a sudden order to ride be given.

All Sapphirehold's female warriors had adopted the finely woven metal mesh caps that were part of every woman fighter's gear to secure their hair lest it should loosen and serve some enemy as a handhold in battle.

She had changed from a linen to a wool shirt in deference to the autumn chill. The garment was an old one and pulled somewhat where it was fastened over her breasts. Its color was the green commonly used by the partisans because of its camouflage value.

Eveleen liked green anyway, he thought irrelevantly. She had been wearing very nearly this same shade when he had first seen her that day three years ago she had sat her future students on their rears on the pistol range.

He was close to her now, and his pace quickened. She seemed withdrawn and pensive beyond her usual wont, so much so that she did not become aware of his approach until he softly spoke her name.

Riordan looked up quickly, in surprise. She recovered herself as swiftly, and, smiling, motioned for him to join her.

He settled himself near her. "You're gloomy this morning," he observed.

She nodded. They had proven sensitive to one another's moods almost from the time they had begun the active phase of their mission, perhaps because they had to work so closely together, all the while preserving the secret of their origins. He had caught her properly, and it was rather too late to cover herself now. "The Ton-heir fought off a wardwolf threatening the does the night before last."

He looked at her in surprise. "That's no mean feat for a boy barely nine years old."

Her great eyes sought his. "Ross, Conroc's a child, a child who's not permitted to be young. I don't mind so much for us or for most of our comrades, either, but I hate the thought of those babies having to become men and women before they ever have a chance to know what it's like to be children at all. . . . I sound like a total idiot, I suppose?"

"No. I didn't have such a hot time as a kid myself and know . . ." Ross frowned and fell silent a moment before going on. "They deserve a better break. At least, we can start hoping they might get it fairly soon."

The man waited until his companion had finished eating before broaching the subject of their war in earnest. When she set her plate down, however, he straightened in the manner she recognized to mean that he would speak to her as commander to his chief officer. "Did you give any further thought last night to what we'd been discussing?"

"No," she admitted contritely. "A bed's like an opiate after several nights on the ground, and I jumped into mine almost immediately. I did mull it over a little this morning, though."

"That's more than I can claim," he confessed. "With what result?"

"Nothing significant. There are no real problems that I can see, just the detail of scheduling. We might as well put it all to the others and let them help with that."

He laughed softly. "An excellent suggestion, Lieutenant. I've no great desire to take it entirely on myself, either."

The council was quickly convened and included both the higher officers and their lesser aides, all those who commanded raids, even the smallest forays.

The latter people were most important now. It was their commander's intention to keep a number of teams within the lowlands at all times, small groups that would be able to conceal their presence even under greatly increased patrol activity and yet be large enough both to maintain contact with potential targets and to release couriers at regular intervals to keep their officers apprised of their position and other pertinent developments.

In order to meet the challenge of these reports, at least one of the five units into which the partisans had long been divided would have to be ready to ride at an instant's notice, and each of the others was to be prepared to move with little more warning, leaving a sufficient force behind to serve as a home guard and to form a large strike force with any of the others should a situation warrant massed effort.

Many of those present groaned aloud when they heard those orders. The volume of work evolving on each of the Sapphireholders and particularly on these, their leaders, would be greatly increased even if there were little or no comparable growth in enemy activity in the lowlands. That was not likely. All of them shared Murdock's belief that Zanthor would have to act more aggressively if his hopes were to survive the coming winter by very many weeks.

Their hearts were light despite that and despite the additional danger they knew they would have to face. Ross had succeeded in communicating his certainty that victory in the foreseeable future was just about inevitable. Hope in the return to the long-neglected working of their domain fired their hearts like good wine. They were prepared to face whatever must be endured to secure that infinitely desired goal.

12

THE WEEKS THAT followed proved even more demanding on the partisans than they had imagined when they had embarked on their commander's intensified campaign, but they were also many times more rewarding.

Murdock had not misread the course his enemy would take, had to take. The Ton of Condor Hall strove desperately to strengthen his hard-pressed army against the ever-more-virulent assaults of the Confederates and against the steadily approaching winter. He used every tactic available to him. Large convoys; small, rapidly moving units; crushingly heavy guards; independent, frequent patrols; decoys; and, above all, frequency of shipment—all played their part in his massive effort.

Some, much, did get through. An astonishing amount did not. The invaders assuredly would not be weaponless before their foes or reduced to fighting as infantry, nor would they freeze or starve in the snows, but both men and springdeer should be well chilled and very lean by the time spring came to relieve them, enough so to reduce their energy and capacity for battle and to leave them with but scant love for the man who had hired their swords and had then failed to provide adequately for their needs.

So the Time Agent was thinking to his satisfaction when a courier tore into the camp.

He and his officers were beside her even before she slid from her steaming wardeer. "What news?" he demanded.

"Columns, Captain, two of them. The first is a deer herd, maybe two hundred head, and is probably meant to draw us. It is moving carefully and swiftly but lowers its caution every now and then, as if it wants to be seen. Also, it is rather lightly guarded. There are no more than thirty riders with it in all, including the herdsmen."

"The second?"

"A convoy. Twenty-five wagons. Two hundred guards plus drivers. This one travels very secretly indeed for all its size, and it is only by chance that we discovered it."

"Their locations?"

The woman bent to study the map of Sapphirehold's lowlands which Ashe had brought out upon her arrival and which he now spread on the ground before them. "In the same general quarter, but they are well apart."

She pointed to an area of softly rolling hills, the gentlest part of the embattled domain and once Luroc's prize pasture land. "The herd is coming through here. It is making very good time, and if we want to strike it, we shall have to do so quickly."

"Naturally it is making good time," Allran growled, a scowl marring his features. "That was always perfect country for spring-deer."

"A trap?" Murdock asked. "You say they appear to be trying to lure us."

"Away from the convoy, I believe. The terrain is too open for a second party to be riding secretly near enough to it to provide aid in the event of one of our sudden assaults. We have scouted all the area around it and have found nothing."

"They could be depending on speed to get them through should they escape trouble in their role as decoys," Eveleen interjected. "A herd like that, unencumbered by baggage or wagons, can move very rapidly."

"That's probably precisely their intent and hope," Murdock agreed.

He turned once more to the scout. "The convoy?"

"Here." She indicated a location within, as she had said, the same sector of the domain but which might have been on a different continent for all the similarity the two regions bore. The route it followed was through a broad range of heavily wooded hills so steeply pitched and rugged as to be almost miniature mountains.

Ross's brows came together. "That's not easy ground for wagons to negotiate."

"No, but neither would they logically be expected to attempt it, and the trees do help muffle the sounds of their passing. Then, too, their escort is a large one and appears to be giving a good part of its effort to aiding the train's progress."

"Outriders?"

"We have not seen any, but I can give no assurance that there are none. The countryside offers too good concealment, and I was sent to you very soon after our discovery of it. The others may have found something since my leaving them."

The partisan commander studied the map intently for several minutes.

He raised his head. "Eveleeni, Allran, summon your divisions. Gordon, order mine to saddle up. We ride in force."

"After which one?" the Dominionite officer asked curiously.

"Both."

Ross smiled at their expressions. "If we start now and travel fast, breaking our journey only long enough to keep ourselves and our mounts fit to fight, we should meet with the herd here by dawn tomorrow."

He touched the map with the point of his sword. "That will put it about parallel to the convoy's route and as close to it as we can expect them to come if they both hold to their projected courses.

"We'll sweep down on the deer from these two points, completely encircling the herd and its guardians before we actually force battle.

"Our greatest danger is that they may be able to break through with a stampede charge, but by closing the net quickly and moving into range at once, we should be able to depend on surprise and on our own numbers to give us possession of the animals without too much difficulty."

"The guarding and delivery of so many springdeer will drain us rather heavily," Eveleen noted. "Will we have sufficient warriors left to go after the convoy?"

He glanced at her. "Good point. You got me on that one. We'll bring enough riders from Korvin's division to fill that need."

Murdock turned back to the map. "After they're safely off, we move east. Four hours' hard riding should bring us to this place. It's right on our second target's present line of march but well in front of them. Once there, we should have time enough to catch our breaths before we confront them."

He looked up. "I can't be certain of all of this, and we'll have to see the lay of the place and the train itself before we finalize our plans against that. Maybe we'll only be able to take part of the convoy or maybe we'll miss it entirely, but only time and closer contact will tell us that. For now, Comrades, let's ride!"

13

THE SUN HAD just lifted over the peaks of the ever-present mountains when the Sapphirehold force reached the site where their commander had chosen to await their enemies' appearance.

They were weary after their long ride, but warriors and mounts alike were well used to the demands of the life they led; their ability in the coming battle, the coming battles, would not be lessened by so little.

Ross had so positioned his troops that neither those with him nor with Eveleen on the slope opposite them had to contend directly with the sun's bright glare as they watched the northeast for sign of their target.

Minutes passed. Perhaps the herd had gone by already or had altered its course and would avoid this place altogether.

The partisans stiffened. There it was, cresting the tall rise capping the valley to the north and spilling down its gentler southern slope.

Gordon looked once upon his partner. Even after some of the other coups they had pulled off since taking to this life, he still felt something akin to awe in this moment. Murdock's calculations had not varied from the reality of their foes' arrival by more than three minutes. "Sometimes, I think you're more Hawaikan Foanna than Terran Time Agent," he said softly.

The other's eyes danced. That was high praise coming from Ashe, who had not viewed the strange trio's extrasensory abilities

with the same suspicion and discomfort as had his younger partner. "I'll thank you not to call those ladies down on us, my Friend.
The thought of them spooks me worse than Zanthor I Yoroc and
all his mercenaries."

His words, light in tone as they were, had been spoken in a
voice pitched scarcely above a whisper, and he said no more after
that.

All speech faded, and the partisan ranks fell into total silence.
The invaders were still too distant for even normal conversation
to betray the ambush had they been traveling quite soundlessly
themselves, which they patently were not. The noise generated by
their own movements would be sufficient to deaden the invaders'
senses to considerable carelessness on the part of the concealed
fighters, but wariness was by then part of the Sapphireholders.
They would not voluntarily do anything that might betray them.

The familiar battle tension surged and ebbed and surged again
along Murdock's nerves, but despite that and with all his intense
concentration on the Condor Hall riders, his heart leaped up within
his breast. The sight of so many slender deer moving together,
unbound, with all the grace and glory of their kind was enough to
stir the blood of any man.

The Condor Hall riders kept their charges traveling at a good
pace, and they were not long in advancing up the valley.

Every partisan seemed to freeze in his saddle, watching, ever
watching. There would be no horn signal this time, nothing that
might give a moment's additional warning to those below.

When the lead riders reached the point the war captain had fixed
in his orders, they would move.

Soon. Very soon.

Murdock's fingers touched Lady's neck. She leaped forward,
effortlessly lengthening into her flawless gallop.

His command moved with him. A double column of riders
flowed down into the valley from the slopes on either side. They
did not engage their enemies at once but rather continued their

wild race until their target was completely encircled. Only when this was accomplished did they close with the invaders.

Now the reason for the dual column became evident. The inner line alone sought contact with the Condor Hall warriors. The others maintained their position, ready to hold the deer should they begin to run.

It was a tense enough job and an important one. If those animals succeeded in breaking free to scatter in the valley and the hills nearby, most of them would be lost to the partisans and their allies, or else all thought of taking the convoy would have to be abandoned. The task of collecting them again would require too much time.

They were not called upon to act. The loose springdeer were frightened, but they were fairly tightly massed, and the uneven action of the fighting pressed them, first in one place, then another, keeping them milling and uncertain of course rather than encouraging a stampede in any one direction.

The battle itself was extraordinarily short lived, scarcely longer than the attackers' charge. The invaders were at too great a disadvantage to maintain their opposition for long. Their surprise had been complete, and the number of warriors so suddenly come against them considerably exceeded their own.

Above all, they had little desire to continue this fight. They were angry with Zanthor I Yoroc for his use of them. Even had their officers not informed them in high dudgeon that they were riding as lures to draw and keep Sapphirehold attention away from the wagon convoy, they were not stupid men and would have soon come to realize that fact themselves. The studied carelessness that had marked their conduct during the whole of this mission would have declared it quite clearly enough. Mercenaries like themselves rather than the men of Condor Hall had borne the brunt of the war after its opening blows had been struck. Their own unit, though not long come to it, had already given good service, and they resented being cast away in this manner, delivered up, as it were, to their enemies' swords.

So be it, then. They had been all but given into this trap, and they were not inclined to make a useless sacrifice of their lives now, not when it was so well known that the Confederates did not treat their prisoners as did the Ton who had hired them. They cast down their arms and sued for peace.

The Sapphirehold leaders examined the captured herd critically.

"He's been buying deer," Eveleen remarked, "and has been going far afield for them. A full quarter of these were never bred in this region."

"They come from the forests far to the northeast on the Mainland," Allran informed her. "We often see them at the fairs when we bring our excess stock over for sale."

She studied the strange steeds. They were large and heavy of body with proportionally big heads. "Are they wardeer at all?" she wondered aloud. "They're not quite the size of drays, but I can't imagine riding such clumsy-looking creatures."

"They are far from clumsy, Lieutenant, and yes, they do battle service, although I grant that they lack the speed and agility we require in our mounts."

"I don't think I'd find it very comfortable sitting one of them for any length of time," she observed. "What kind of people use them?"

He smiled, trying to imagine her diminutive form astride one of the big deer. "The foresters who normally ride them are huge men, very tall and mightily muscled. The biggest in our company would scarcely be of middling size among them. They want substantial mounts under them. Speed is not really possible in their endless treelands, and so they value it little, whereas they do want strength and the ability to work their small fields and bear heavy burdens long distances. Theirs is not deer country, and they did not enjoy the luxury of having even two breeds near to hand, so they concentrated on developing this one to serve both their saddle and dray needs."

"What'll we do with them?"

"They look like good animals whether they suit our purposes or not," Ross interjected. "Gurnion should find their strength very helpful, particularly for servicing his foremost lines where they might occasionally be pressed into actual battle duty as well."

"What about the rest?" the archeologist asked him.

"We'll keep no more than a third of them, fewer unless the quality's exceptionally high. The winter could be a bad one. No use in risking putting strain on our feed stores by bringing in too much new stock at this point."

"Ton I Carlroc will profit well by our day's work in that event."

Murdock seemed to lose himself in thought for a moment. He recalled himself quickly and smiled. "Not Gurnion. Let all but the foreign animals be delivered to the mercenary camp. Give greetings to Commandant A Murdoc and say that these captures come to him with Firehand's compliments."

He laughed softly, guessing their thoughts. "It's a bit of bravado, maybe, but I want to establish Sapphirehold's place beside the Confederate domains in A Murdoc's regard. We might otherwise suffer when the time comes to divide the spoil that'll result from this war."

"He would cheat us . . ." Allran began in anger.

"Hardly. Officers with a reputation for doing that don't get many new commissions, but neither do mercenaries lightly surrender hard-won gains to those not fully earning them. That's why the Commandant must be made to understand completely our heavy and long role in all this."

No one questioned that Jeran A Murdoc had the power to disrupt the distribution process if he chose to do so. A column such as he led would not have hired itself without the promise of a strong spoil share as well as the gold it contracted to receive.

The weapons expert shook her head. "I think Sapphirehold will be as fortunate to have Firehand on its side in those councils as it now is to have you managing its battles," she said in admiration.

"If our employers lose, we lose, Lieutenant," he replied, somewhat embarrassed.

Allran gave him a strange, sharp look. "Right now, any dividing of spoil seems vary far away."

"With a lot of hard fighting ahead before we get there," Ross agreed.

He straightened. "Mount up. There's a convoy lonely for our attention. Let's not disappoint it any longer."

14

_____

SOON, THE CAPTURED springdeer and the carefully interrogated prisoners were ready to depart.

The main body of the partisans waited until they had passed out of sight before moving themselves. Murdock tried never to permit any prisoner, no matter how seemingly secure, to observe anything that might give a clue as to his intentions or probable direction of travel.

He scowled now as Eveleen swung into her saddle and brought his doe close to her so that they might ride together. "Why are you using Comet instead of Spark?" he demanded bluntly; he had noted her choice of mount at the outset of their mission, but there had been no appropriate opportunity to challenge her then, and he had forgotten the matter until now.

The woman bridled under his tone but controlled her response. "Because Spark picked up a stone on the last raid. It bruised his hoof."

"Sorry, Eveleen," Ross apologized after a moment. "I should know better than to question your judgment, and the choosing of his steed is each warrior's business."

"Don't worry about it," she replied, "but I am curious about your dislike of Comet. He's a fine animal."

"I know, but he's no match for Spark." He glanced at the way before them. "We depend so heavily on our deer. I don't like the thought of your coming into possible danger through some imperfection . . ."

He shrugged. "As you say, Comet's as sound as any of the other springdeer we have."

Little was said during the next several hours. The raiders were tired. They had ridden far and had fought one battle already this day, and they knew another faced them at their new destination, or faced them if their leader had read his enemies rightly and had plotted and timed their movements accurately.

The change in the nature of the land announcing that they at last were nearing the proposed attack site came rather suddenly. The hills became higher and steeper, rougher and more difficult to negotiate. First brush and then stands of trees dotted the slopes. These increased in density and frequency until they formed a full, thick cover over all the land.

The convoy had been sighted in a long rift bisecting the range and tracing its full length as if Life's Queen had drawn a mighty knife along its backbone before the stone had frozen into its present solid form.

Ross had reasoned that this would remain the invaders' route. It was direct, and they would be able to travel it without having to contend with any excessively rough places. Besides, once upon it, he did not see how the party could quit it. The deermen could readily have scaled the slopes bordering the natural path to go their own way, but the clumsy, presumably well-laden wagons were another matter. They were fairly bound to keep to the rift after they had started upon it.

True, it was conducive to ambush, but the same could be said of every part of the Sapphirehold lowlands, and they would be counting on secrecy to shield them, that and the size of their party. They would not disqualify the rift for security's sake.

The Time Agent was not very pleased with that road himself and was even less pleased once he reached it and had to come to a decision as to their course of action. It was too narrow and the surrounding terrain too rough to permit the ambush he had hoped to set, one allowing a quick sweep by his entire force, striking every part of the long line simultaneously and breaking it swiftly. There was no stretch along the whole course of the great fissure sufficiently free of almost perpendicular cliffs and deep drops to permit such an attack. He would have to modify his tactics and hope no heavy price would be exacted for that compromise.

Murdock chose what he believed would prove to be the best place possible to meet the convoy, and settled down to wait. His force was nearly a third greater than his intended victims'. Even if he failed to take all the deermen and, therefore, could not chance delaying to bring the supplies away with him, he could be fairly certain of at least stopping the wagons long enough to fire them, provided they came this way at all.

His order of battle was simple enough. Allran's division waited at the far side of a sharp, cliff-walled bend. When the first part of the Condor Hall column reached him, he was to leap out on it. Ross's unit would be waiting, well concealed, farther back along the trail. When the sounds of the charge reached them, they would strike at the rear or at whatever portion of it was before them should the train be uncommonly extended, trapping the bulk of it between them. The remaining partisans, those under Eveleen Riordan, had been divided, part going to the front, part to the rear positions. They were to act as flying squads, giving aid to the other officers as needed and trying to prevent riders from the convoy's center from either breaking and fleeing or from racing to the aid of their embattled comrades.

Ross sighed. It was as good a plan as conditions and his own ingenuity permitted him to devise. If fortune were with them, total victory should be theirs. If not, the battle could be a costly one.

His expression hardened.

It might never come to battle if their enemies went by some other road.

They had been waiting here three hours now, better than that, a good two hours longer than he had anticipated. There should not be such variation from his calculations. The herd might have shown this fluctuation, but not wagons. They were capable of only so much speed either in spurts or during sustained effort, and he was too well practiced in considering both factors to err very greatly now.

The undisturbed ground testified that they had not already passed, but perhaps they had chosen another path after all. Perhaps one of them had merely broken down. Disabled vehicles could not be left behind here, for those coming after would not be able to go around them and would have to be abandoned as well.

Maybe they were just traveling a little more slowly than they might, realizing they would lose more time to broken wheels and axles in such country than they would by showing the care needed to prevent accidents in the first place.

He drew and released a long breath. The convoy was coming at last.

Silent progress through this terrain was impossible for that number of wagons despite the thick growth of trees, and the partisans could hear the sounds of their approach long before the first of the advance guards rode into view.

The invading warriors looked tired and sweaty despite the cool autumn breeze whipping through even this low place, and both faces and clothes were much grimed. Their journey thus far had not been an easy one.

Ross's heart seemed to slam against his ribs. If they were detected now, or at any time in the next few minutes before Allran was ready to make his move, they would have a hard fight ahead of them, numerical superiority or not.

The Terran's eyes were silver ice. The wagons were rolling by, each drawn by four good drays, each separated from the next by mounted warriors. These last looked as trail-worn as the deermen leading the convoy had been, but like them, they were alert and rode with their hands on their swords. All wore the Condor Hall insignia.

Bad news. These men would not break or cast down their arms

as had the mercenaries riding with the herd. Zanthor intended that this shipment should get through.

Ross's head raised in the old, defiant manner. He would see to it that it did not.

The minutes crept by like weeks. Would the lead riders never reach Allran's position?

It came then, the familiar, every-terrible clamor of battle—the shouts, the curses, the screaming of frightened dray deer, the clash of good steel against steel.

The first sounds of it had scarcely reached his ears before he sent Lady Gay forward. The partisans spread out along the narrow front of the rift riding rapidly to encircle the rear guard.

Because of the nature of the place, each party found itself more or less equally matched in numbers in the first moments of combat before all the attackers were able to reach and engage their targets. The invaders had apparently realized this would be the case if they were attacked and had prepared themselves to take advantage of that fact, for they responded with amazing swiftness not only to fell as many of their foes as possible in the time thus given them but to block the narrow road against them so that only a limited number could come at them, however many had begun the assault.

The tall cliffs lining most of the way helped their cause. There was only a slender shoulder where the rift met the advancing rock, wide enough to give passage to a few deermen and yet be easily defended by equally few.

The Condor Hall warriors had both courage and skill under arms. They neither sued for quarter nor gave it, and it was a long, bloody time before the partisans at last began to batter down their defense, longer still before they could work their way along the line of wagons, most of which had been turned to block the road.

Every foot of ground was bitterly contested, but at last, the two Sapphirehold forces met, trapping the few remaining defenders between them.

There was no call to surrender, no suit for peace. The surviving invaders fought grimly on, determined to sell their already lost lives as dearly as possible.

The flow of battle brought the three Sapphirehold leaders near one another as they struggled to bring down the handful of invaders still under arms, Eveleen and Allran so close that they might have served as shieldbearers for one another in a different kind of warfare, the commander a few yards from the other two.

The weapons expert fought like a spirit of retribution, a cold, precise fury ever hunting the hot blood of those who sought to rip land and life from the people she had come to love. It was always thus with her, and the partisans had not long begun their war before Condor Hall's warriors had learned to hate and fear her terrible skill and the intelligent courage driving its use even as they hated and feared her more famed leader.

The one she now faced recognized her. He would have preferred to engage some other, lesser foe, but, since fate had given this task to him, he was determined to come away from it with her life on his sword even though he must perish soon himself. He believed his skill to be the equal of that, however good she might be.

He lunged, intending the thrust to be a feint to draw her guard and open her to a second, more deadly stroke.

His springdeer slipped as his arm drove forward. The blade, instead of streaking toward the woman, pierced the neck of her mount.

Comet reared in pain and terror, then fell heavily, throwing his rider and pinning her beneath him.

Allran felled his opponent as the agent's wardeer gave his death-scream. He turned in time to see Comet go down.

With a cry of rage, he swung at the invader who had done this thing, striking him full in the breast. So fierce was his thrust that the sword pierced him through the breadth of his body, and the mortally stricken warrior was flung from the saddle as if he had

been hit by a catapult-fired stone, taking his bane-weapon with
him.

The Lieutenant leaped to the ground. There was no danger now
in this area, except for the terrible, crushing weight upon Eveleen's
fragile body.

Several of the other partisans, also freed from combat by the fall
of their final opponents, raced to his aid. Together, they raised the
slain wardeer and drew the Terran free.

Murdock's opponent crumpled before a trust that had seemed no
more than a flickering quiver of his blade. One more invader
remained, but Gordon and another of the Sapphireholders moved
in to take him before their commander could offer challenge, and
he found himself free at last of death's grim shadow.

He turned to scan the suddenly quiet battlefield.

Ross paled as though fatally stricken himself. Allran was nearby
on his right, bending over the still form of a woman. Her chestnut
hair pinned in its golden net and the starkly white, wrenchingly fair
features were all too clearly visible to him. Several of the others
were with them, but his eyes were so fixed on the two Lieutenants
that he could not have named them.

Shock seemed to freeze the heart in his breast. Not this, he
thought, desperate with fear and anguish. Anything to him, but
not this. Not Eveleen.

Lady Gay reached the pair in a moment.

Murdock was out of the saddle before the doe had ceased to
move.

The kneeling man looked up. His face was grim. Grief and anger
at his own helplessness were etched on it. "Comet fell on her. She
has just ceased to breathe . . ."

"Get out of there!" The Time Agent flung himself on Eveleen,
all but hurtling the other aside.

He covered her mouth with his, pinching her nose with his left
hand so that none of the air he forced into her should escape that
way.

He felt her chest expand, paused, drove the air from it, filled her lungs again. Ten minutes went by. Twenty. He was growing exhausted himself when he thought he heard a soft moan.

Imagination?

Ross sat back on his heels. No, her breasts rose of their own accord.

Before he could move to aid her further, Eveleen's eyes opened to look into his. They were puzzled and unfocused for a moment but then widened in horror as memory returned to her.

"Gently!" he said quickly. "It's all over now."

"Comet?" she asked faintly after a brief silence.

"Gone. He died almost instantly. I'm sorry for that."

"You wronged him," she whispered. "This wasn't his fault . . ."

"I know," the man responded, "but be quiet now. Please. Gordon's here. Let him look you over."

She nodded her assent, and the commander arose, giving place to his partner.

Ross found everything in good order, as he had known would be the case.

The frenzied activity that always followed a capture was still much evident, for the convoy was a large one, and each wagon had to be carefully searched and all possible stores loaded on the captured deer. The remainder would have to be burned, although he hated to let it go; the wagons were too slow, too cumbersome, to risk traveling with them himself.

The wounded claimed a great deal of attention. There were many both among Sapphirehold's warriors and the invaders, a number of whom had been stricken three and four times before giving over.

Some of the injured hung between life and death, and Ashe had been forced to devote his first attention to these rather than to Eveleen. Murdock had fought off her initial peril, and the withdrawal of Gordon's aid in the immediate aftermath of the battle would have cost the lives of a number of the others. Only when he had finished with them had he been able to relieve Ross and concentrate on the injured Terran.

Once the commander had assured himself that there appeared to be no unanticipated difficulties in the aftermath of their victory, he sought out Allran and drew him aside. "I'm sorry for the way I used you back there."

The Lieutenant shook his head. "Forget it. What you did, I should already have been doing."

"And so would you have done had I given you another moment. Shock freezes us all. It was only some kind of instinct that moved me so quickly."

The other smiled faintly. "Eveleeni has reason to praise that instinct."

"If she's not hurt inside," he responded bleakly. "She won't have gained much if she's only to die slowly now instead of painlessly, as would have been the case if I hadn't intervened."

That thought had been in the Sapphireholder's mind as well, and he nodded glumly. "Perhaps Gordon will be able to give us his verdict shortly."

Ashe came to them a little while later. He could tell them nothing definite. It was his belief that the Lieutenant had not suffered any permanent or grave injury, nothing, in fact, beyond an incredible bruising, that shock and weight had been responsible for the failure of her lungs, not any damage sustained by them. He was almost certain there had been no breaking or crushing of bone, but more, he simply did not know. Only a much closer examination than he was able to give her and several days of careful observation would tell him what he needed to learn. Until then, until her body had proven itself sound, she must be regarded as one of the more gravely wounded despite her protests that she was fit to ride or to fight as need demanded.

15

A T LAST, THE partisans were ready to depart. They divided as was their custom, some going south with the bulk of their spoil and the captives, most returning to the highlands, bringing with them what they desired of the captured stores and, of course, their own wounded.

The shock of the accident was not quick to release Eveleen, and she was more than content to ride the litter despite her words to the contrary, a fact not lost upon her commander to his ever-increasing concern.

It was the worst journey Ross Murdock had known in a long time, that return to base, as bad in its way as the terrible flight downriver in Terra's past with the Baldies close on his heels. He had known fear then and despair and physical pain and exhaustion. Now, his lash was uncertainty and a dread so sharp that he could have become sick with it had the strength of his will been less.

The Sapphirehold force pressed on hour after hour, long after darkness had fallen. With so many of their party incapacitated, a number of them totally, Murdock had no desire to meet with a company of the enemy following after them to avenge either the herd or the convoy. Only when the weariness of his warriors and mounts threatened to become a danger in itself did he finally permit a halt.

Dawn brought no easing to his heart. One of the wounded had died during the night, and another remained stable but very close to death.

Gordon's report on Eveleen's condition was essentially the same, but he was more guarded in giving it. She was having pain, a considerable amount of it, and he could not as yet say whether it was born of the tremendous battering she had taken or from more grievous cause, although he hastened to assure his comrades that he had found no other symptoms of internal injury, which by rights should be revealing themselves if anything existed to spark them.

Ross's head lowered as Gordon spoke. He tried to allow himself to be reassured, but his despair only increased. Ashe really was good, a near miracle worker to the minds of their Dominionite allies, but comrades had died despite him, men and women who would have lived had they had a real doctor or a proper hospital in which he could treat them. The same lack could all too easily kill Eveleen Riordan within the next few hours or days.

The partisans started again with the first light, not slackening pace even when they entered the highlands once more, nor did they halt a second time until they were within their home camp.

Ross waited only long enough to see that his wounded were settled before going to Luroc to make his report.

As was his wont, the Ton did not interrupt his war captain during his account, nor did he speak at once after it was completed. Murdock had left little for him to question, and, in truth, he would have been loath to press for further detail now even had he wanted it. The warrior looked totally spent.

The agent was sitting in his usual place. His head was lowered, and his shoulders were uncharacteristically bowed with the weight of his weariness and with something that was akin to defeat. "I brought you a costly victory," he said suddenly after a long pause, speaking with apparent difficulty. "We have eleven slain and forty wounded, twenty-four of them seriously even—if Eveleeni proves not to be so. Those are the heaviest casualties we've suffered since taking to these mountains."

The gray eyes seemed utterly stripped of life when he raised them. "I should have guessed what that convoy would do and allowed for it in my planning. It was the very course I myself would've followed had I been in their place. If you no longer want me as your commander, I'll resign . . ."

"Do not be a fool! Do you imagine yourself Life's Queen's equal that you should ever be able to read the minds of men? You succeed quite often enough in doing it, or in seeming to do so."

I Loran looked at him then and sighed. "Your pardon, Rossin. You have enough riding you without my adding to your burdens."

Ross compelled himself to straighten. "You're right. I was being the fool, and yet, I can't but grieve over our losses both personally and because we can so ill afford them. It's a commander's duty to keep such to a minimum, and right now, I can feel only my failure to do that."

"Without cause, as your own reason must tell you. Naturally, we suffer for those who have gone down, but we must expect losses when we deal with Condor Hall's own warriors rather than with mercenaries. Zanthor has them too filled with tales of the revenge we shall exact upon them and their kin in the event of Confederate victory for it to be otherwise. Your party met with a large number of them and paid the cost of taking them, a cost far lower than might well have been expected.

"As for Eveleeni's fall," he added shrewdly, "that was accident, beyond any human controlling. Save that a sword caused it, she could as readily have gone under her deer in the training field or during a supposedly quiet ride."

The black eyes gentled. "It is you who gave her a chance at life."

"That means nothing if . . ."

"It means everything."

Ross's head bent once more but raised again in the next moment. "Thank you for that," he said quietly.

The Terran gave his companion a wan smile as he literally willed the depression to lift from him. "You make a strong advocate, Ton Luroc."

"I must be to argue down so unbending an opponent. Firehand

meets with no such condemnation from others as he levels against himself on occasion."

The pale eyes twinkled now. "I've heard Luroc I Loran speak as harshly of himself."

"And have named him a buck's tail to his face! At least, I have never gone so far with you. . . . Ah well, have I not said before that we are both stubborn men?"

The Sapphireholder settled back in his chair. "No one in Gurnion's camp will be minded to slight you when your latest donation arrives." He shook his head. "That convoy was a prize even beyond the gold. Blankets, winter clothing, medical supplies, foods designed to sustain men and beasts in bitter weather—all costly material, and much of it is not readily procurable. Zanthor will be hard pressed to assemble another shipment like it in any reasonable time, and all the while, he will be galled by the knowledge that he will have no better guarantee of getting it through to his army when he does put it together than he did with this first lot."

"He must try." Murdock sat forward. "I've been thinking, Ton. Suggest to Ton I Carlroc when you next meet that he keep his army at least partially active during the coming winter while the weather permits it at all. Continue striking the invaders, even if just to the extent of annoying them and forcing them to use more of their stores. The more unsettled we can keep them during the winter, the less able they'll be to meet a full assault come spring."

"That is sound," the older man agreed, "but I want you there to press your argument yourself. We meet in council in a fortnight, and with the crisis coming upon us, Sapphirehold's war commander should be present along with the others, particularly since we now have mercenaries to face as well."

The Time Agent nodded. "It would be best to coordinate our efforts as much as possible," he agreed.

The energy was draining out of Ross again now that their more pressing business was finished, and all the weight he had borne earlier returned to crush his spirit.

He glanced at the door. "With your leave, Ton Luroc, I'd like to see how Eveleeni's doing . . ."

"You have my leave to go to bed. . . . No, I try to restrain myself from issuing orders to you, but upon this, I do insist. The call to battle could come again at any moment. You are but poorly fitted to lead warriors now and will be less so in a few hours' time, perhaps incapable of it altogether, if you waste the chance to rest now. Besides," he added bluntly, "there is nothing you can do."

Murdock stiffened.

Luroc half softened, half laughed. "You do not like to hear that, my Friend, but the truth of it remains all the same. . . . Go to bed. Good news or bad, it will reach you quickly enough when it breaks."

16

THE TIME AGENT slept like one dead, and when he did at last awake, he saw by the position and intensity of the light streaming into his room that it was already past noon.

He sat up with an oath. Even normally, there was too much to be done in the aftermath of a raid to permit such squandering of precious time. Now . . .

He was just pulling on his boots when Gordon's knock announced his presence.

Ross looked up at him a little crossly. "Have you spy-holed this place?"

"Not at all," he replied cheerfully. "I was just glancing through the paperwork on your desk and heard you stirring."

The war captain's eyes swept his quarters and then returned to his partner. Everything was in its usual place, his gear restored to battle condition, yet Ashe had ridden the same mission with him and had unquestionably spent most or all of last night with the wounded. His strength, or, rather, his staying power, seemed almost superhuman. Still, it could be abused. "It seems that I've managed to take advantage of you again."

The other smiled and shook his head. "Not at all. I'd slept a little the previous night. You'd held the watch."

The younger man steeled himself. Fear was a burning spear in his heart, although his friend's easy manner reassured him somewhat. Gordon would surely not be speaking so lightly now if death had claimed any more of the wounded or if its grim shadow lay on Eveleen Riordan. "Were there any fatalities during the night?"

"No. There won't be now. Even Jorcan is past his crisis."

"Eveleen?" he asked, unable to restrain himself any longer.

His terror was apparent to the other. Gordon's fingers pressed into his shoulder. "She's all right, Ross. There's no more danger."

Murdock's eyes closed. He had braced himself for disaster, but relief threatened to overwhelm him, and it was a moment before he could trust himself to speak. "Thanks, Gordon," he whispered.

He drew a deep breath and collected himself. "She's conscious?"

"Our Lieutenant has been awake over an hour already," Ashe informed him.

"Why wasn't I called?" he demanded angrily.

"Because, hard as this life can be, I'd prefer not to be severed from it for a while longer. Neither Ton Luroc nor our fair comrade would have looked kindly upon me had I roused you before you'd slept yourself out."

"She can have visitors?"

"Naturally." He eyed Ross critically. "Since this much time has lapsed already, you might want to take a little more to eat and polish yourself up a bit. If you show up looking like you do at the moment, she'll take it that she's definitely not long for the world, whatever my assurances to the contrary, or else she'll think that something awful's happened. Besides, she needs time herself. Marri's still helping her get fixed up."

Murdock's fear returned in full force. "What do you mean helping her? What's wrong?"

Gordon laughed. "Calm down! She's stiff and sore as hell. You'd be, too, if a springdeer had just crashed down on top of you."

Ross flushed but accepted the rebuke with good grace. "After breakfast, then. . . . Are the rest up?"

"A few. Most're still sleeping, or were when I came in."

"Anything to report?"

The archeologist shook his head. "No. There was no other action while we were gone, and nothing of significance happened here. Everything on the desk can afford to stay there a while longer."

The war captain waited until he felt a decent amount of time had elapsed before going at last to the cabin occupied by his chief officer.

He paused for a moment in the door of the single room comprising the small dwelling, although Eveleen had been quick in granting him leave to enter.

She was sitting up in her bed, her back supported by pillows, her magnificent hair spread out like a veil around her. Seen thus, she seemed more like the distant, royal daughter of some powerful Ton than the fiery and able partisan officer beside whom he had lived and fought these last fierce months. She also looked vulnerable and impossibly fragile.

He willed himself to overcome that last feeling and moved into the chamber, all the while studying his Lieutenant intently.

Her small face was still too pale, making the eyes seem even larger and more luminous, but it was quite unmarked.

That was apparently not true of the rest of her body, for she wore the shirt serving as her bed robe fastened tightly to the throat, and even so, he could see a finger of dark brown extending up the right side of her neck from beneath the collar. He shuddered in his heart at the sight of it, knowing how easily such a bruise might have become a break.

She read his thoughts and laughed. "I'm told I shall live, Firehand. Come here and sit down if you have the time."

The man was quick to obey, drawing up the chair already placed by the bed so that she need not strain or turn to look at him. "How do you feel?"

"Sore."

Her hand went to her hair. The movement was oddly slow, as if it troubled her greatly to make it. "I couldn't even have managed this if it hadn't been for Marri's help."

"That'll pass off soon."

"I sincerely hope so!" she responded with no little feeling. "She'll give me no peace until it does."

"You'll just have to court patience, Lieutenant," he told her unsympathetically.

"I don't seem to have much choice in the matter."

He smiled at her expression. "It won't be for long. I hadn't expected to find you looking so well. Or so pretty," he added, believing she would be pleased to hear that after having suffered what could all too easily have been at least a temporarily disfiguring accident. "You're quite beautiful, you know."

The woman laughed. "From the neck up. The rest of me makes quite another vision!"

Her expression softened suddenly, and she held out her hands to him. "There's no way for me to thank you for what you did, Ross."

His fingers closed over hers. "Having you warm and alive before me is thanks enough, Eveleen Riordan." Murdock's grasp tightened. "I said I had no wish to see you in danger. Now I realize how much I meant it."

He felt embarrassed and carefully lowered her hands, slowly, so as not to further jar already tormented muscles. He released her but kept his fingers close to hers. "Lieutenant Riordan, as a favor to your commanding officer, the next time you decide to fall off a springdeer, please don't insist on bringing him down on top of you."

She responded, as he had intended, with a grimace and an exaggerated shudder. "No fear of that, Lady Fortune willing!"

Her bright eyes fixed him. "Well, Captain Firehand, what did we gain for all our trouble?"

He described the contents of the wagons.

Eveleen smiled to hear that report. She was no less aware of the value and significance of those goods than he was and would have entered into a detailed discussion of their future course had her chief permitted.

Murdock rose to his feet. He feared to tire her by remaining too long and already thought her face seemed a little more pinched than it had been when he had come in. "That'll hold. Rest for now. A few days will give us both time to consolidate our thoughts. We can talk about it then."

She had to content herself with that, and after learning the fate of their other comrades and exacting his promise to return as soon as his duties permitted, she bade the gray-eyed man farewell.

17

THE TERRAN WOMAN remained in her quarters that day and the next but after that felt sufficiently free of stiffness and discomfort to return to her normal duties, all save combat, which neither Murdock nor Ashe would permit this soon after her fall. Sapphirehold was not so desperate for warriors as to require or chance that.

There would have been no need for her to ride even had the opposite been true. The days following the raid were quiet with no activity from Condor Hall and nothing to call the partisans away from their mountains save the seemingly endless patrols scouring the lowlands.

They used the time well. There was work to be done in the camp which had been, if not neglected, at least not given its proper attention while the press of battle had been so heavy upon them. Both this place and the watch posts guarding the few passes were examined and refitted where necessary to meet the assaults of the fast-approaching winter, whose bite was now to be felt, at times keenly, in the sharp, high wind, and care was taken that those in the noncombatants' village lacked for nothing that might be provided to ensure their comfort and safety.

The officers met frequently as well. Ross had not merely been offering Eveleen comfort when he had promised to speak with her within a matter of days. All knew that the closing weeks of this year and, to an even greater extent, the opening ones of that to come would be crucial to the war's outcome. As far as was possible, they wanted to anticipate their enemies' moves and lay their own plans for countering them.

There was opportunity in plenty for rest, too, thrice welcome after the weeks of strain and almost constant effort just gone.

The war captain was no less glad of those hours of ease than were the soldiers he commanded. He passed many of them with Ton Luroc, whose company he thoroughly enjoyed, and many more with Gordon and Eveleen.

Especially with Eveleen. Once he had recognized and acknowledged his feelings for her, he had begun to look at her, to study her, with different eyes. What he found left him both amazed and not a little ashamed that he had remained oblivious to it all for so long.

Eveleen Riordan had always been closely guarded about her deeper thoughts and feelings, he realized now. She had to make her way in a world quicker to challenge than to welcome her, and she had set her defenses early both to shield herself and to keep her strengths and plans concealed before those who might conceivably be prepared to use too intimate knowledge of her against her.

Like everyone else willing to observe and judge her fairly, he had not been long in recognizing her competence, her courage, her good humor and ready wit, her gentleness both as a companion and a woman, but she had always before screened much of her inner life, most of what went on behind the facade she chose to present to the universe around her, and he had allowed himself to remain all but blind to its very existence.

Now, she was drawing back some of those thick veils. He began to see a little and guess more of this hidden part of his comrade and chief officer, glimpses of a strange, bright spirit that ever more powerfully intrigued him. He wanted to delve its depths, even though instinct warned him that he would never be able to fathom them completely.

Eveleen was helping him. Such was the trust that she was giving him that she who was so proud and independent acknowledged her need for closeness in this alien world and time. She went so far as to permit him to see when shadows occasionally weighed her heart, although of these shadows, she never spoke directly.

Darkness seemed to grip the weapons expert almost openly on the afternoon she first took to the saddle again after her accident.

Ross did not at first press her, but he began to worry as time went on without any brightening in her attitude. There was something troubling her, and he wondered if it might not be nervousness over traveling mounted again. A fall such as she had taken could readily have induced fear.

By all appearances, Eveleen Riordan seemed quite free of any such difficulty. She sat Spark easily, with no sign of tension, but that might too easily be meaningless. The weapons expert's courage and iron control were sufficient to mask even stark panic.

Perhaps it was not this at all, but whatever twisted in her heart and mind, he longed to bring her ease, if only that of companionship and sharing.

"You're doing fine," the man began tentatively.

"Yes. There's only a little soreness left."

She looked at him suddenly. "You thought I might be afraid to ride? Is that why you just about ordered me to let you come with me?"

He flushed. "The possibility had occurred to me," he confessed. "I didn't mean to insult you."

"You haven't," she assured him quietly.

The brown eyes remained on the war captain. Their expression was grave and also tender. "You're quite a man, Ross Murdock."

She tossed her head then so that the long braid confining her hair danced upon her shoulders. "We've come a long way. Let's top that rise there and then rest a while."

So saying, she put Spark into a quick canter that moved them well in front of her companion.

He asked similar speed of Lady Gay, but the buck had a good lead on them and reached his goal before they again came up to him.

The two riders dismounted, letting their reins hang down as a signal to their animals that they were free to browse but were not to stray from this area.

It was a beautiful and rather unusual place. The crest of one of the lower peaks, it was unlike most of its fellows in the range in being quite narrow, no more than seven yards across at its crown. Murdock mounted the rise to its crest. His heart swelled when he gazed out over the incredible world below him.

All that a wild and unutterably fair nature could create in such an area was there in front of him: mountains, hills, sharp, deep valleys, well nigh all thickly forested save where an odd patch of moorland or cliff or waterway broke the expanse of the trees.

Lakes were a common feature of the region, small in surface area but incredibly deep and blue like liquid sapphires—it was from their abundance and startling color that the domain had taken its name. They were cold enough to give pain to anyone drinking their clear waters too quickly. The streams feeding them ran free and fast, frequently erupting into rapids or dropping suddenly into almost too beautiful falls.

Beyond all this, framing it, were the higher spires of the range, many of them forever bearing brilliant, cruel crowns of ice.

The Time Agent knew this place well. He had come here often since he had discovered it early last spring, had come to think through a difficult maneuver, had come when the need for peace or beauty or grandeur was on him, had come more rarely in happiness and in hope, and always, he had found what his spirit sought.

He had never spoken of its existence and had never heard any other mention it, and although he realized his Sapphireholders must have known of it as well, he had always secretly hoped none of his comrades was touched by this mountain crest as he was.

Now, however, he found he did not grudge the exquisite woman beside him even this, that, on the contrary, he wanted to lay it before her as one would lay a precious jewel at the feet of a goddess.

He turned to her and then smiled. The same exaltation he experienced in this place was on her as well. What he wished to offer, Eveleen Riordan already knew.

More than that. He realized with a start that in suggesting they rest here, she had been giving it to him.

"You come here often?" he asked.

Her nod did not surprise him. "You're no stranger to it yourself, Firehand?"

"No."

An air of quiet gravity settled over her, and she gave a little sigh. "This really will be our last winter up here?"

"Very likely."

He studied her intently. "Don't you want peace?"

The surprise in her expression gave him her answer even before she spoke. "With all my heart! These people need to be able to live and work like they used to do. They're ordinary folk, you know, most of them, however good they are at this business fate's forced on them."

"You're good at it, too."

The woman nodded briskly. "I know the weapons, and Zanthor I Yoroc is an enemy easy to hate. Every blow I strike cuts into his heart's desire. I just wish they could slash into his heart itself."

"Why, Eveleen?" he asked softly, startled by the vehemence with which she had spat that last out. "This isn't our war, not really."

She looked at him, her eyes grave, measuring him, before she made her decision to respond with the truth. "I'm making up," she told him, "doing for these people what I can't do for my own."

Eveleen walked a few steps away from him and fixed her eyes on the panaroma below. "Ever since I learned about the Project, that time travel is not only possible but accomplished fact, I've wanted to go back, undo the centuries of wrong my race has suffered."

Murdock said nothing, and she faced him once more. "I know that's not possible. I wouldn't do it if the opportunity were offered to me, with the most extensive possibility and probability scenarios of the results giving me the all-clear. It's bad enough playing God and altering the history of other worlds, but I couldn't take any such chance with our own. I wouldn't dare."

She shrugged. "The people of this island are facing the same kind of trouble mine did, a vicious, powerful tyrant trying to take their lands and slaughter their leaders and everyone else with any superior gifts. It's a privilege to be able to serve them, to do for them what I'm powerless to do for my own."

Her head raised. "Have I succeeded in damning myself?"

"No. I trust you."

Eveleen's expression softened. "You're no neutral in this yourself. No one's blind to your love for Sapphirehold."

Murdock nodded. "I'd give my life and my soul to bring this domain through, and after my experiences with the Foanna, I know enough to mean precisely what I say."

"It's appreciated, Ross," she told him. "Gordon once said to Luroc that his people would go through a wall of fire for him because he moved to protect them when he learned of their danger. So they would, but they'd go through a league of it for you, on their knees if need be, and that includes I Loran himself."

He smiled but shook his head. "They come close enough to it as it is. There's always danger when we ride . . ."

Suddenly, his eyes brightened. "I could remain here, Eveleen," he said quickly, before his courage failed. He wanted to share the shadow-hope Gordon had awakened in him, that and a newer one, but if he did not speak now, uncertainty and embarrassment would silence him again. "I could make it. My share of that gold we took plus what we contracted for in exchange for our services here would let me start up a small company. Firehand's reputation should draw men to me, and I wouldn't be surprised if a few of my Sapphireholders, especially among the women, won't be all-fired keen to go back to their old lives, not after discovering what they can accomplish. They'd ride with me as well. I might conceivably wind up a full Commandant before I'm through."

"It's not impossible, Ross," she said quietly. "In fact, I'd say it was probable."

Murdock drew a deep breath. He had gone so far. Now, he must face the rest of it. "Would you stay with me?"

The brown eyes met his. Eveleen Riordan was no child. Their expression was certain and steady, although surprisingly somber for such a moment. "Yes, I'll stay, or I'll go back with you if that's what you finally decide to do."

That was it, quiet and matter of fact. He stared at her, not quite believing that she had consented, until her soft laugh made him feel very young.

That broke the spell. Ross came to her, folded her in his arms, kissing her deeply and savoring her response.

At last, Eveleen gently drew back. "Patience, Firehand. We're going to do this properly, with everything in its right order."

"Why doesn't that surprise me?" he grumbled, good-naturedly since anyone knowing the weapons expert as well as he did could have expected nothing else.

She smiled. "I've always been a great respecter of tradition, not to mention a lover of ceremony. I really wouldn't like to be done out of this particular one."

He kissed her again, tenderly this time rather than passionately. "We'll see if we can't arrange something to your liking as soon as we get back to the camp," he promised softly, with great happiness.

18

THE PAIR'S ANNOUNCEMENT of their intention to wed was greeted with great glee by their comrades but with little surprise. The following evening, they made their vows before the priestess of Life's Queen who served Sapphirehold in accordance with the custom of the island and the continent beyond it.

Dominion's Goddess seemed to smile upon their union, for they were granted the opportunity to enjoy and accustom themselves to it as day followed day without trouble or activity from their foes.

The time flew by almost too quickly for Ross. The day when he and Luroc must depart for the Confederate council was fast approaching, and he wanted to be very certain of his wife's complete recovery. He had to be. Hers would be the command and hers the responsibility for the Sapphirehold complex until they returned. If she was not fully able to bear it, another would have to be given the task in her place.

He need not have worried. She still bore the fading bruises she had sustained, but they no longer hindered her movements. The partisans would be well led, whatever they might have to face.

The Ton's party left at dawn on the appointed day. The journey would be a long one, four full days, although they would be moving quickly and utilizing the mountain trails known only to Sapphirehold's defenders.

Murdock sighed in his heart as they drew out of sight of the camp. Though the time ahead should be peaceful enough, he dreaded it, knowing what it would cost Luroc.

l Loran was not fit for such a trek. Even if the weather held steady, he would suffer. If it broke at all, he could come into actual danger.

Ross's mouth hardened. These four days would not be the end of it, either. The conference, however cordial, could only be a strain in itself, and then would come the return. He could only hope it would not all combine to overwhelm the ruler's already meager store of strength.

His concern for the older man had moved him to ask Gordon to accompany them. If something did happen, Ashe's skill as a healer would make him worth any ten others to them.

Besides, he wanted his partner there. Ross was always nervous on the rare occasions when he was forced to attend one of these conferences. There were too many chances of his making some mistake and giving them away, and the possibility of error would be even greater at this one with a high-ranking mercenary present. He wanted Gordon's moral and practical support.

Twelve rankless warriors completed the unit. The three leaders could have traveled this route alone since it was not in itself difficult for those knowing and understanding its ways and the chances of meeting with any of the invaders were almost infinitesimal even while approaching or leaving the Confederate camp, but the Ton judged it best to ride escorted, as custom dictated. With an end to the bitter war at last visible in the foreseeable future, the nuances of politics must be ever more carefully observed.

Despite the Terran's concern, their journey south passed without incident or difficulty.

Luroc endured his pain without complaint, and although he was white-faced when he was lifted from his springdeer at the end of each day, he was able to greet the following dawn with his strength and vigor apparently restored.

Because of the effect the heavy traveling had on their Ton, the Sapphirehold party chose to break early and pass the fourth night in the mountains rather than press on immediately for the Confederate camp, judging it best to approach their allies when their ruler was fresh.

The sun was well up when they started out. Neither Murdock nor I Loran had any desire to startle the outlying sentries unduly, although the arrival of the other Tons and their chief commanders would have told the army that some major conference was imminent.

The guards were indeed surprised to see the Sapphireholders suddenly appear from out of their highland stronghold. They were not slow in offering challenge all the same, but the green and brown colors favored by the partisans were well known to them, and Ton I Loran had been often enough in their camp before this that they recognized him now. They gave him and his party courteous greeting and passed them through without further delay.

For the first time since their departure, the Sapphireholders felt a twinge of concern for their safety. Unlikely as such a meeting might be, all knew how easily an army's outer lines might be breached by a daring band, and none of them had any wish to confront such a unit out of Condor Hall at this point, not with an important mission before them and a man incapable of either battle or rapid movement as the one who must carry most of it.

No danger presented itself. They passed through the main pickets and then the actual camp sentries to find themselves in the midst of the huge southland army.

The sight of it was enough to take the breath of the Sapphirehold warriors and that of the off-worlders as well.

Neat files of tents stretched out on every side to the limits of vision in this hilly country and beyond. Soldiers, animals, equipment were everywhere to be seen. Their numbers and the apparent abundance of their supplies were all the more astonishing in the face of the fact that this was but part of the Confederate force: the rear guard, the marshaling troops and those returning for a brief rest from the front, the commander's personal guard and, now, those of the assembling Tons.

There was no sense of threat on any of them. This place was guarded by the mountains and by the Sapphirehold partisans holding them and was in no danger from the fighting that raged so fiercely nearer the Corridor. Only almost total disaster to the southern forces battling there would permit such trouble to come upon those stationed here.

Many eyes turned to the small unit as they rode between the tent rows. At first, these glances were only mildly curious, but they quickly became intensely so. It was not usual for the Sapphirehold war captain to attend council here, but neither was this his first time in the great camp. Some there knew him, and word spread rapidly that Firehand himself had come down with his partisans.

The crowd thickened until Gordon frowned to see so many pressing so closely upon them. A spy or a traitor could too easily be lurking among all these men, and there was a high price on his partner's head.

Ashe issued a curt order, and the soldiers behind him moved forward to form a living screen around their leaders.

The Ton of Willowlands had been watching the newcomers from the entrance of the great meeting tent. He stiffened at the maneuver, understanding full well what had sparked it. Their quickness to respond to a potentially dangerous situation and even more so their devotion to their commanders impressed him powerfully, and he swore mentally that his failure to foresee this possible threat had forced them to make a display of it.

Gurnion ordered his troops to fall back out of bow range, then mounted his own springdeer and hastened to join the Sapphirehold party.

As soon as he drew near enough, he extended his free hand to clasp Luroc's.

Ross gave him salute and then dropped back a little, allowing the two leaders to ride together. His own attention was fixed elsewhere. They were near the meeting tent, and he saw guards stationed around it, men and a couple of women wearing the black uniforms that proclaimed them mercenaries.

These, too, were watching him closely, although they did not give their curiosity such open play as did their allies.

His head raised. He need not feel ashamed of the company in which he rode or of the rough clothing he shared with them. His effort and theirs had made it a proud uniform.

He and Gordon were the first to dismount when the party reached the tent's entrance. They hastened to help I Loran from his buck and to ready the crutches he must use to propel himself.

Murdock did not even think to wonder what impression this service might make on the grim-faced sentries. Luroc I Loran was so worthy and fine a man that showing courtesy to him was not merely a kindness but a duty and an honor.

He accompanied the domain ruler inside. Their comrades made no attempt to follow, knowing this was to be a meeting of Tons and commanding officers only, but he did not doubt that the Sapphireholders would remain close to the tent until their leaders emerged once more. His partisans were proving uncommonly protective of what they considered to be their own.

Ross saw that the others were all present.

That was to be expected. Because of the difficulties travel caused him, the Ton of Sapphirehold preferred to arrive last at these gatherings, though always on time, conduct the business at hand as quickly as possible, and then depart again as soon as he might. He disliked being away from his people too long, and his pride rebelled strongly against making any greater display of his infirmity than was absolutely unavoidable.

Ross's eyes swept the assembled Confederate rulers and the mercenary Commandant they had hired.

Jeran A Murdoc was there, of course, a tall, black-uniformed man with a heavily jeweled swordbelt and a plain-hilted, businesslike weapon slung from it.

His features were long and thin, more like those of the Terran's than like any to be found in the northern part of the continent or the islands surrounding it. Despite that fact, Murdock breathed a sigh of relief that he had not attempted to claim kinship with the famed officer, for Jeran's complexion, hair, and eyes were all the deep black needed to combat the powerful light Virgin poured on his homeland.

The pale eyes rested pensively on I Loran. Had the Ton been putting him to some sort of test?

The ruler of Willowlands, as commander of the Confederate army, repeated his greeting to Luroc of Sapphirehold, this time voicing it formally in the name of all his colleagues.

He turned to the Time Agent. "You are welcome to our tents as well, Captain A Murdoc. As ever, you have our congratulations for your successes and our thanks for all you have sent us, and my personal congratulations and grammercy as well."

"Thank you, Ton I Carlroc. Sapphirehold is always pleased to advance her allies' cause." The other Tons, some of whom had known I Loran since his youth, offered him their personal greetings, then all repaired to the great round table which had been prepared for their use.

Ross waited until Luroc settled himself and then took the chair to his right.

The Ton holding the place directly opposite them, a heavy-set, arrogant-looking man in his late middle years, frowned deeply.

Sapphirehold's master saw his look and stiffened, his eyes flashing dark fire. "Captain A Murdoc holds those mountains secure which now shield this camp. If you would have only one of us sit with you, then, Ton, it is I who must rise and stand behind his seat!"

The other man flushed and looked away.

Gurnion rose swiftly to his feet. "Peace, Ton Luroc, and you, Captain. Two places were prepared for Sapphireholds' representatives. This council has need of both your opinions."

Luroc nodded and allowed his body to relax. He did not envy Willowland's Ton the task of controlling and working with his large number of independently minded colleagues and was glad he had had the wisdom to keep apart from the Confederacy itself even while allying himself with its cause.

There were no further difficulties. I Carlroc gave a report of the war effort as it now stood and stated his opinion that a change, a slow fear, seemed to be growing in their enemy's mind and heart, that if they laid and worked their plans well and fortune were at all with them, they might see an end to the war during the year to come, or at least, see an end to the worst of the fighting.

He turned to Ross, who echoed the Confederate leader's hopes, then stressed his belief that it was essential to keep as much pressure as possible on the invaders, harrying them right into the winter until the weather grew so severe as to forbid any war activity.

Ross's eyes caught and held each one of them in turn. "Understand this," he told them gravely in conclusion, "we'll win, or we should, but we'll have to fight as we've never fought before once we do succeed in bringing them to bay. Zanthor will have to release his Condor Hall hosts then, and they war with a fanatic's fire."

He frowned. "No. You nod, but we of Sapphirehold have met them in battle; you haven't, not in any number. Everything, all the hard, bitter combat your soldiers have endured until this moment, is nothing more than a testing, preparation for what you're going to face when you join at last with them, however greater your numbers might then be."

"Are they your friends that you praise them so highly?" one of the lesser Tons asked testily.

Ross eyed the man coldly. "They're my bitter and hated foes," he answered evenly, "but I'd degrade myself and my comrades and I'd be allowing you to hold a false security for which you'd pay heavily later on if I spoke otherwise of them. Whatever we think of their leader and cause, Condor Hall's own troops are brave men and brilliant fighters, and they'll yield to nothing but death or unconsciousness."

"The condition of those you send us is proof enough of that," Ton I Carlroc said bitterly. "What a waste, what a criminal waste, of good fighting men!"

"In a way, their tenacity shouldn't amaze us overly much," the agent told him. "They've got kin whom they love, and Zanthor has been careful to school them in the belief that we'll return slaughter for the butchering that accompanied his first, seemingly undammable advances. They have no reason to doubt him considering their own ways, and he keeps them well segregated from his mercenaries, who would soon deprive them of any such delusions."

That should have been the end of it, but to Ross's disgust and growing impatience, the discussion dragged on, seemingly interminably on. Every one of the Confederate Tons believed their foes were at the end of their strength and resources and that spring would bring them an early victory. Murdock's warning that it could still prove to be a costly one failed to check that enthusiasm or their ever-sharpening interest in the spoil they hoped to secure at the close of the war. Most of them resisted the idea of spending any more of their resources than they now felt to be essential to keep what they held to be an already broken enemy in check until the final kill.

Jeran A Murdoc caught his eye at last and shrugged, but the Commandant, too, had enough talk about treasure that was patently not yet won. "Condor Hall still has mercenary columns and its own garrison," he said abruptly, seizing the opportunity to speak that was presented by a momentary lull in the debate. "No victory is guaranteed until it has been gained, most assuredly not this one. I suggest that we bend ourselves to harrying our foes as far as we can into the winter as Firehand suggests and leave the division of Zanthor I Yoroc's lands and goods until we have actually taken them from him. Slacken off now, and it is all too conceivable that he might yet make himself ruler over yours."

19

ALL THROUGH THAT morning and the afternoon following it well into the early evening, the meeting continued. At last everything that could be planned and arranged, everything that could be countered, so far in advance, had been considered and resolved, and the weary leaders arose, spent in mind and spirit as a warrior is spent in body after long hours of combat.

Ton Gurnion would not hear of the Sapphirehold unit's departing from his camp so late in the day and insisted upon pressing on Luroc the use of his own tent and arranging for others to be set up near it for the rest of the party. For all his pride, the exhausted I Loran was glad enough to accept the offer.

Ross accompanied the Sapphirehold ruler to I Carlroc's big tent. They discussed how their partisans might most effectively increase the pressure on Condor Hall's supply lines in the crucial weeks ahead, then the Terran asked permission to join Ashe in the quarters assigned to them. He, too, felt as if he had passed the day in battle.

To his surprise, I Loran shook his head. "Stay a while," he said. He looked pointedly at the camp table near the tent's entrance. "Gurnion was good enough to leave us some of his wine."

Murdock carried the light table over to the Ton, then filled two of the goblets arranged around the decanter. One he handed to Luroc and took the other himself after drawing a chair close to the ruler's.

He rolled the pale liquid on his tongue. It was a fine vintage, light and very dry.

A smile flitted about his lips. It was not so long ago that he would not have recognized how good this was. The appreciation of wine was another of the benefits he had reaped from his association with Gordon Ashe, over and above the opportunity to range time and space.

Luroc sipped his portion, his eyes closing in pleasure. "It seems like a weary age since I last tasted anything the equal of this."

"Soon now you'll be in a position to import quality goods again," his companion promised, "or reasonably soon."

"I know. I must just court patience. We cannot expect Zanthor I Yoroc to supply us with prize stock, and I cannot in conscience consider squandering our resources on luxuries at this point."

He took another sip and settled back in the chair, letting it take his weight. "You did well in there," he told Murdock.

"So did you." Anger flashed momentarily in Ross's eyes. "I'd have flattened you if you'd actually tried to get up and give me your place."

The Ton chuckled. He enjoyed the younger man's directness of speech. "There was never a fear of it," he assured him. "Gurnion I Carlroc would not have allowed such an insult to take place."

The Ton's dark eyes studied Ross somberly. "I did fail on another point. I knew Commandant A Murdoc would be present, and I still let you walk in there dressed like a herdsman."

Ross only shrugged. "I can survive our kind of war dressed like a herdsman. I mightn't fare so well in something fancier."

The eyes still held him. "True enough, but half a high officer's or a ruler's time is spent in political maneuvering, and for that, the trappings are important. You will have to learn that lesson, Rossin A Murdoc, if you are ever to command a column successfully, as I believe you shall gain the right to do within a few more years. Your work with us has gone far toward preparing you for the responsibilities of major rank, and if you will it, you are likely to attain it soon."

The agent looked away. "As you said, we need our resources for necessities right now, not luxuries. To my way of thinking, uniforms fall into the luxury category. Those mercenaries should be able to see that."

"For the war itself, yes. A council like this is another matter." Luroc sighed. "No one blames you, Rossin, but Jeran A Murdoc now thinks less of Sapphirehold, less of me, for providing so poorly for you. I saw the look he put on me. You have done too much for my domain for any form of neglect on my part to be tolerable."

"The Commandant can take his opinion and . . ." Ross began hotly.

"Again, my young Friend, this is politics. It is also a rebuke for a fault I myself have owned for a long time. I do owe you, Rossin, for more than I shall ever be in a position to repay. . . . Be silent for once and let me finish! You would try Life's Queen Herself at times."

"Go on," Ross replied, uncomfortable but knowing enough to keep his mouth shut.

"Your contract will be fulfilled and your loan repaid, and there will be more besides beyond your spoil share, but it cannot be what I of my own heart and honor would give. My first responsibility has to be to my domain. Sapphirehold will need the bulk of its resources and the bulk of my personal fortune to regain its prosperity even with whatever recompense comes to us with the victory. War's blight does not simply vanish from the battleground with the cessation of hostilities."

The Ton straightened. "Bring me that saddle pack over there. The black one."

Murdock complied. Luroc opened it and took a leather-wrapped package from it. This, he handed to Ross. "Your belt is too plain for anyone but a raw recruit, and it is worn besides. Let Firehand hang his sword from this instead, at least while he is in the company of strangers."

The Terran's breath came in a hiss when he folded back the wrappings. What he held was a belt, all right, one set, every part of it, with matched emeralds, each of remarkable size and perfection.

"This—this is too much," he managed at last.

Luroc's voice was oddly soft. "No, that it is not."

The Ton's usual manner reasserted itself. "Had I a second son, this would have been his portion. There is no cadet in my house, and my heir cannot claim what would have been his right. I would have you take it now and stand for me in the place of that other son." His tone gentled once more. "I am pleading as well as giving, Rossin. Can you refuse me?"

The younger man's head lowered. "No. You read me right. I can't."

Murdock fastened the belt about his narrow waist, first stripping his scabbard from the discarded belt and transferring it to the new one. The plain, worn sheath did not detract from it. This was a tool, not a toy, and in time of active war, it was expected to be utilitarian. None of the others in that council had borne anything more ornate, whatever their richness of dress in other respects.

"Much better," Luroc I Loran declared. "See that you show yourself wearing it tonight, for a while at least, even if you are tired, and wear it until we get back to our own camp."

"I will with pleasure, Ton," he agreed, smiling.

Luroc continued watching him. There was a difference in his scrutiny now, and Murdoc looked at him, puzzled. "Ton?"

"Sit down, Firehand."

He obeyed, concerned now by what he heard in the domain ruler's voice. "What's wrong?"

"I was fortunate I had that belt," I Loran said, as if he had not heard the question. "Otherwise, I should have been hard pressed to come up with a suitable gift that you would be able to bring with you when you return to your own."

The Time Agent's heart gave an ugly jerk, but he made himself frown. "I'm an independent. You know I'm not attached to any of the columns."

"Not any of those on the Mainland or the islands near it," he agreed. "You were never born in the regions my people know, or if you were, your race most certainly was not. When I said just now that you would soon be ready for a major command, I did not imagine it would be over soldiers of any realm familiar to me."

"Just what do you mean?" Murdock was scared, but he forced himself to direct that emotion into the show of anger appropriate to the situation had he been innocent.

The older man chuckled. "I traveled extensively in my youth, Rossin A Murdoc, or whatever the name you actually bear should be. I never came across a people the like of you and your two associates. That rock ferret's face of yours did not come from any northern or middle portion of the Mainland, and your pale skin eliminates the far south as your place of origin. Since there are three of you, all apparently unrelated, you can't excuse your differences by claiming some strange mixing of blood. You are strangers, all of you, as alien as if you rose from the depths of the sea or out of the ground beneath us."

"If you believe that, why have you . . ."

"Do not credit me with too sharp a wit. It was a good while before I realized I could not place you, and it took longer still to convince myself that my seemingly wild surmises were correct."

"What do you expect me to say, condemn myself or call you either a liar or a madman?"

"Say nothing. I know you will not betray those who sent you or their reasons for doing so, and I do not want to see you foresworn before me."

Murdock started to unclasp the belt, but the Ton stopped him. "The gift is genuine. You and your comrades have more than proven yourselves our friends. I spoke now to warn you. I was a blank shield before I fulfilled the dream and married into Sapphirehold. The belt was my groom's price . . . That early experience with war rendered me more able than my colleagues to believe in the danger Healer O Ashean proclaimed, but the breadth of knowledge I had gained about my world helped open my eyes to your strangeness. You will be dealing with other mercenaries now as well as with the Confederate Tons, and you will have to treat with them ever more frequently and closely as this conflict draws to a close. Take care how you conduct yourself with them and warn Gordon O Ashean to be on his guard as well if you do not want to be forced to declare who and what you are before us all."

"What about you?" Ross asked, neither confirming nor denying his companion's allegations but giving his curiosity full play. It was inconceivable that the on-worlder could have divined the actual truth, but he had to know how close to it he had come. "Who do you think we are?"

I Loran shrugged. "Life's Queen alone knows. I myself do not believe that the Mainland is the only large landmass on this world, and there are the old tales of strange travelers. It does not matter. You have stood well for Sapphirehold, and I have seen enough of all of you to know that your care for us is genuine, though at the start, it may be that your purpose was merely to oppose Zanthor I Yoroc."

He sighed, as if mourning a loss he knew must come. "You and your comrades have nothing to fear from me, Firehand, now or in the future, whether you go or stay in the domain you have fought so hard to preserve. As I said, I spoke only to warn you."

"We thank you for that," Murdock responded slowly. "False or true, such a tale would breed distrust and fear. The Confederacy can't afford either in its ranks at this point."

Luroc smiled. That had been a good thrust. "Answer me one question, Rossin, and then I shall have mercy and allow you to escape. Did you accept the belt out of policy or for love of me?"

The Terran's eyes fell. He was, in fact, hurt. "For love, Ton."

"In that spirit, too, was it given."

Ross's gray eyes met Luroc's. "Was it also a test?"

"One with the background you claim would have known the stones, but, no, it was not. I was sure enough of my deductions not to have to degrade my offering. You three are very good in your roles, but we are thrown closely together in this life. There have been many little points significant to someone already suspicious enough to watch for and read them."

Ross Murdock left the ruler's tent. He felt as battered as if he had taken a physical beating. He paused a moment to orient himself.

The partisan standing sentry duty started to raise his hand in salute, but it stopped in midair as his eyes fixed on the jeweled belt. They widened, and his mouth dropped open.

In the next instant, he gave a great crow of delight that quickly summoned the remainder of their company.

The reaction could not have been more excited or more jubilant, and Ross cringed at the magnitude of his failure to recognize these gems.

He realized something else as well, and a glow of warmth filled him. A mercenary served for gold. He could expect no more than gold as his reward, and he could expect to have no significance in his employers' eyes beyond whatever respect his battle skills and tactical abilities might earn for him, that and, hopefully, human concern for his physical welfare. This greeting, this joy with and for him in his advancement, was dramatic proof of how much more he had found in the hard-fighting domain whose cause he carried.

Ashe managed to rescue Ross from their enthusiastic troops after a few minutes and just about dragged him into the tent assigned to them. "What in all the levels of time has happened?" he demanded once they were alone.

"I seem to have gotten myself adopted as Luroc's cadet son." He licked his lips. "He knows us for aliens, Gordon, or at least for strangers."

The archeologist said nothing for several minutes after Murdock had finished his account of all that had happened in the ruler's tent. "It was only to be expected, I suppose," he said wearily at the end of that time. "As I Loran himself pointed out, we've had to live too closely for too long among these people. It was all but inevitable that we'd give ourselves away eventually."

"Maybe," the other agent responded bitterly, "but we could probably have pushed it back a good while yet if you'd kept command of the mission. . . . Damn! I was with him so often . . ."

"What else could you have done?" his partner asked mildly. "You're his war commander. You had to confer with him and associate with him. Actually, I'd probably have done much worse. My mind and temperament don't mesh as closely with his as yours do."

"What now?" Murdock pushed his feelings of guilt to the back of his mind. Their assignment was still not quite completed. Until it was, its conclusion could not be considered secure, but they dared not stay to finish it if by so doing, they would be putting Terra in peril. Should they publicly betray themselves, should the story that off-world humans had intervened here reached the Baldies, their own homeworld could well be seared into another lifeless cinder, a mote for the dead Dominion whose fate they were fighting to avert.

"Precisely what Luroc told you. Carry on as usual. That Ton's an old fox. He's not going to risk the war's outcome or jeopardize Sapphirehold's future position. He's given us our warning, and you very smartly shot one back at him. We'll all have to leave it at that."

"You trust him?"

"Don't you?"

Ross nodded. "Yes, I do, but . . ."

"But nothing. That adoption business was apparently real. That's our answer as to I Loran's intentions."

Murdock touched the jeweled belt. Suddenly, his expression darkened. "I'll be able to keep this, won't I, because I'm not bringing it back just so some brass hat can hang it in a museum or on his wall."

Gordon smiled, recognizing the old Ross Murdock in that. "As I've said before, there's no rule against souvenirs. Just slip it under your clothes when you make the transfer and don't say anything about it. . . . Of course, your wife might want to make a necklace out of those stones."

"She's not getting them, either," he said, smiling as well.

"Thanks, Gordon."

Ashe stood up. "On your feet, Firehand. I believe your instructions are to show yourself wearing that belt, and I imagine our comrades are going to want to celebrate your promotion. You'll have to go along, but for heaven's sake, don't let them get you drunk. Three stiff shots of some of these local concoctions would be enough to put any uninitiated Terran under the table."

"Trust me on that one, pal. After today's interview, I'm not likely to put myself in the position of accidentally saying anything to anybody not of our select little team."

20

WHEN THE PARTISANS reached the mountains once more, they found their outposts' excitement no less keen when they were informed of their commander's new status than had been that of Luroc's escort, although it was expressed more quietly out of deference to their position and responsibility.

The Ton was eager for his own quarters after the long journey, but he had not been slow in noting his people's response to their war leader's good fortune, nor had he missed the slight lifting of Murdock's head when he had received their congratulations, and he drew rein just outside the Sapphirehold camp. "Take the lead, Rossin. This triumph is all yours."

"That wouldn't be right, Ton Luroc . . ." he began in protest.

"Custom be damned, Firehand. Our warriors see your success as their own. Let them have the joy of it."

I Loran had not misread his soldiers' reaction, and it was some time before the cheering stopped in the usually still encampment. If Ross Murdock had entertained any doubts as to the regard with which he was held here, this day's events would most assuredly have set them to rest.

Eveleen watched the enthusiastic reception without taking great part in it. She waited until the party had dismounted and each of the leaders had gone to his quarters before seeking Ross out.

She knocked at the door of what was now her cabin as well and then went inside. Her husband was sitting at his desk, already beginning to attack the neatly piled paperwork waiting there, but he rose quickly to receive her.

She slipped into his arms, kissing him joyfully.

The weapons expert stepped back at last and studied him carefully. Her fingers touched the jeweled belt. "I'm so happy for you, Ross," she told him quietly.

"Everything didn't go quite as smoothly as this would seem to indicate," Murdock told her grimly. He recounted what had passed between him and Ton Luroc plus Ashe's feelings on the subject.

The Terran woman's face was drawn by the time he had finished. "We won't have to take to our heels, not until we're really done here?" she asked sharply.

"As of now, no, according to Gordon. We all want to see the war to its end. As long as Zanthor I Yoroc's still fighting, he remains a threat, and he's nowhere out of it yet." His eyes were bleak. "We'll just have to play it as it comes and hope we'll be able to stick around long enough to finish what we came to do."

"And longer. Sapphirehold can use our help, or yours, in the postwar negotiations. . . . Blast! I suppose we all must've slipped up in a thousand ways since we moved in here."

Murdock shrugged. Crying over past mistakes was useless. For however long they would be left to stay a part of it, they had a war to fight. "It'll take me a couple of days to go through all this. Did anything major happen that I should know about immediately?"

Eveleen shook her head. "There was almost no enemy activity. One of our patrols met and whipped a small Condor Hall patrol, but that was the extent of it. The prisoners taken then should've reached Gurnion's camp shortly after you left it. Otherwise, we had a nice, quiet time of it."

The partisans' delight in the honor done their commander would not be satisfied by a few words of congratulation, however sincerely or warmly spoken. They gave the newly returned riders that night in which to rest but declared that they would celebrate on the next, barring only a call to battle.

None came, and the following evening found music in the camp and an air of general gaiety upon its inhabitants. All were relaxed, and many, particularly among the women, had put on garments they had saved from the time before Zanthor's shadow had fallen over their lives. Apart from the sentries, only Korvin's division refrained entirely from doing so, as they refrained from tasting any of the wine which was otherwise flowing with uncommon freedom, since they had to remain on battle alert.

Ross watched the festivities from the foot of one of the first trees fringing the encampment. His eyes were somewhat somber, for he felt a little depressed by the very lightness his comrades evinced.

This was the way it should be, he thought. These people had a right to be merry, to be able to take and use what was theirs and enjoy the fruits of their labor, whatever they chose to do, not to forever be forced to conceal themselves like brigands on mountain slopes.

Most of them would be very glad to return to the former quiet, ordered course of their lives, to the fields and loom and anvil. The few who would not, who could form the kernel of a superb mercenary company, he could already name. With them behind him . . .

A sudden tightness constricted his throat. The Terran drained his goblet, then filled it again lest someone read his discontent in its emptiness. He was not being left to sit alone for long.

To distract himself, he began to scan the others gathered on the outskirts of the merriment. His eyes came to rest on Allran A Aldar, and he frowned thoughtfully. The Lieutenant had been there a good while now, nearly from the start of the festivities. That was odd, for he was popular with the men and the women of the domain, and he had the reputation of being a fine dancer. He should have been at the center of the celebration, leading a large part of the activities, but instead, he remained thoughtful and withdrawn, seemingly scarcely aware of what was happening around him.

Ross raised his cup again, this time only tasting its contents. Leaving the Sapphireholder to his thoughts, he sought out Eveleen. He spotted her in a moment, sitting beside Gordon and Luroc.

Almost as if she read his thoughts, she glanced in his direction. Finding his gaze on her, she said something to her companions and rose to her feet in a single, lithe movement wonderful to watch.

Carefully skirting the rapidly whirling dancers, she made her way to the place where he was sitting and lightly lowered herself to the ground beside him before he could rise to give her formal greeting.

Her eyes went back to the dancers. "They're so good," she said wistfully. "I used to love to dance. I was good at it, too."

"You're good at everything you do. —Why not join them? It doesn't look all that hard."

Eveleen shook her head. "It's harder than it appears to be. Both the steps and the patterns're intricate, and it's breathlessly fast."

She watched for a few minutes longer and sighed, tempted, but her resolve held. They had no idea how universal these Dominionite dances were, and the team had enough problems as it was without committing readily avoidable blunders.

Ross recognized the considerations that moved her, and his eyes lowered. He felt badly for her and a trifle guilty, as if he were somehow responsible.

He started to raise his cup again but checked himself when he realized that her hands were empty. "I'm a lousy husband. I'll fetch a goblet for you."

The weapons expert held up her hand to stay him. "I've had enough."

She eyed the liquid in his own goblet. "Ton Gurnion sent a supply of his stock back with Luroc. He's been good enough to broach it for the occasion. Would you like some? This home brew's pretty bad."

Murdock shook his head. "No, thanks. Any more, and I'll be getting tight. If our Condor Hall friends start trouble . . ."

"Korvin can handle it. If you're near tight, you'd best leave battle to him," she told him calmly. "Besides, this celebration is in your honor, and we really wouldn't care to have you ride away from it."

She did not press him further when he again shook his head and merely settled herself more comfortably beside him.

They fell into a companionable silence.

The war captain studied Eveleen from beneath half-closed lids.

Her hair was intricately styled, piled high with a braid of pale yellow ribbon woven through it. Her softly fashioned blouse was the same yellow shade and was delicately embroidered with its own thread. Its neck was just low enough to skirt the first rising of her small, firm breasts.

The faint, clean sweetness of the herbs with which she had scented herself rose to greet him as he moved a little closer to her.

Ross had never been so conscious of Eveleen Riordan's beauty, and a sense of wonder filled him that he had been able to win her. He and Gordon might be the only men on Dominion of Virgin capable of appreciating her loveliness, but that had patently not been the case on Terra. He had certainly made no move to secure her favor there; he had been too much of a blockhead to realize he wanted it. It amazed him that his luck had held so long.

"You sounded so sure when you accepted me," he said suddenly. "It took poor old Comet's fall to wake me up, but when . . ."

The woman smiled. "Shortly after we met, as soon as I started to get to know the man behind that burned hand story."

Murdock stared at her. "You never said anything or made any move."

Eveleen laughed. "I have some pride, Ross Murdock! I wasn't about to offer what wouldn't be accepted. You liked me, but you were only looking at an able instructor and at a comrade who was also a pleasant companion. If you'd suspected where my interests lay, you'd have run straight to the first shipload of Baldies you could find and signed on for a long voyage to anywhere."

"You read minds, too?" he growled.

Her smile, her eyes, softened. "I loved you, Firehand. I was aware of the nuances in your response to me."

She glanced in the direction of the Ton and Gordon. "Shouldn't we join them?" she suggested. "If you sit out here too much longer, they'll begin to think something's wrong."

There was a slight question in that last, but Ross shook his head. "I just wanted to have some quiet for a while and to watch everything."

He came to his feet and gave his hand to her. "Let's go keep our host company, Lieutenant."

21

ROSS REMAINED IN camp the following day but returned to the war on the next.

Eleven of the partisans rode with him, his two chief Lieutenants, Gordon Ashe, and eight others. Each carried rations for three weeks, for they could conceivably be gone that long, although the norm for these scouting missions was a little less than half that time.

It would require nearly two full days' heavy riding merely to reach the place where their explorations were to begin, the Time Agent thought somewhat glumly, and once there, they were likely to be kept busy.

His party's goal was the Funnel, the region forming the approach to the Corridor. It was an extremely rough area, close by one of the most impenetrable stretches of the great barrier highlands and scarcely more passable itself in places, comprised as it was of tall, cliff-studded hills so named only by comparison with the giants rising up on either side of them. In any other setting, they, too, would have been termed mountains. They were only lightly wooded, but most sported a thick growth of brush and were otherwise so rugged that they provided an acceptable field for guerrilla work, which the more open Corridor itself did not, a fortunate circumstance for the Sapphireholders in the face of the uncommon amount of activity characteristic of the area.

All south-bound traffic began to converge here. The partisans knew that and came frequently in the good hope of taking a prize.

In order to counter them, or at least to discourage even further depredations, the invaders constantly patrolled the region. The Funnel was too large an area and offered too good cover for it to be guarded the way the Corridor was; its distance from the army would have prevented that even without the difficulties of the terrain. Enemy concentration was abnormally high, though, and the two forces often clashed there, usually under conditions entirely of the Sapphirehold warriors' choosing.

It was his to ensure that the latter remained true if they met on this mission. The consequences of any failure in that respect could be disastrous to his small unit.

As on every other occasion when he had thought about the Corridor and its immediate environs without having some immediate need to lash him, the Terran wished fervently that the Confederacy had been able to move quickly enough to have blocked Zanthor's winning control of it. Had they been able to claim even the passage alone or, better still, some of the area leading into it, life would have been a lot easier for his own small command, if, indeed, the war would not already be ended.

Ross sighed then and turned his mind to more productive work. They could learn a great deal from the signs of the most recent traffic, which they were certain to discover once they reached the Funnel and began examining it, even if they were fortunate enough to see nothing at all of their enemies themselves. He would do well to concentrate on the job ahead of them rather than squander this time regretting a failure long since sealed in history.

The partisans left the highlands early in the day, and although the land through which they traveled still offered them fairly good cover and was not yet noted for the heavy enemy activity they would encounter later, prudence moved them to keep an increasingly sharp guard as they moved deeper into it. Ross halted early that night so they would not have to take their rest in the Funnel itself, but they rose with the dawn and quickly, silently, slipped into the troubled region where their work was to begin.

Signs of enemy activity were not scarce for those skilled enough to find them, and the hearts of all sank a little despite their foreknowledge that this must be so. With Zanthor I Yoroc pushing so hard to get his army ready for the winter and the spring to follow, the partisans realized that warriors and goods were getting though to his lines, but still, all were amazed and discouraged by the amount of material that the tracks indicated was escaping them.

Their leader was no more immune to that dulling of heart than were his companions. It was now obvious that the invaders were likely to be considerably better able to face the challenges of the next combat season than the Confederate leaders anticipated. His allies would have to be apprised of their actual strength, and he pressed his party to discover the full extent of it.

The Sapphirehold unit worked its way down the length of the Funnel almost to the mouth of the Corridor itself before Murdock at last learned all he could of what he wished to know and gave the order to turn for home.

That was a command all of them rejoiced to hear. Although the countryside still provided some cover, it was becoming ever more like that of the Corridor, ever less able to shield them against the eyes of their enemies should any be present to trouble them.

All of them hoped their luck would hold in that respect and no patrols would come upon them. With important information in their possession, it would not be well to enter into any conflict now.

Ross kept his unit moving at a fast pace during the remainder of that day. He always hated missions calling himself or any of his soldiers into this place where they were denied ready access to the mountains and was never sorry to come out of it. Now, the responsibility of the intelligence he carried weighed on him along with the ever-present fear of being trapped here.

The Sapphireholders rode steadily until nightfall. They broke their journey once full dark fell and resumed it again with dawn's first pale light.

They had been riding for some four hours when the partisans spotted a flicker of movement well to the north.

They took cover, vanishing as if they had never been, and waited.

Fifteen minutes passed before the stillness of the scene was disrupted again. This time, there was no doubt. Deermen. They were heading south, riding swiftly without taxing their mounts. The party was small, only six men, and nervous. For all their apparent haste, they were making good use of the cover provided by the broken terrain.

The commander watched them for several minutes as they twisted and swerved in their course so as to keep themselves under the best protection available to them.

They were veterans of this war then. Mercenaries fairly recently come into Condor Hall's service did not move this well. Chance alone had revealed them, and were they only a few miles farther north where they would have enjoyed better cover, they should have escaped detection entirely.

Ross signaled to Allran and three others. "Check them out."

That small party made a tempting target, maybe too tempting. Such had been set to trap him before, albeit never this far south. He would not care to sweep down on them only to find himself surprised by a second, larger force that had been traveling better concealed as a shadow to this first.

The four scouts were gone some time before returning at last with the news that the invaders were indeed alone.

The Terran pondered a moment. His first inclination was to let them go, but Zanthor frequently sent couriers in such small, highly mobile companies, and he could not chance that these carried no directive of interest to him or to his allies.

"Allran, Gordon, take half our number and get behind them. Eveleeni and I'll go with the rest. We should be able to sweep around them if we move swiftly enough."

* * *

The partisans flowed like the waters of a gentle tide through the broken countryside until they reached the place where their enemies rode.

Ross counted the seconds until he was certain his people were all in place, then gave the command to advance.

The sight of the Sapphireholders appearing seemingly out of the very ground with arms drawn and ready to slay was sufficient to cow their outnumbered foes, and the Condor Hall mercenaries surrendered without attempting to draw blade.

The war captain ordered them to cast their weapons aside and then to dismount. They complied at once. The partisans left their saddles as well, and Murdock turned to question the Sergeant who appeared to be the leader of the captives.

A curse, sharp and bitter!

His head snapped about as Allran went for one of the prisoners, sword in hand and poised to strike.

Ross threw himself forward, slamming into his Lieutenant and bearing him to the ground.

There was no struggle. Ashe and one of the others separated the two men and disarmed Allran while their comrades closed in around the captives lest they think to take advantage of the confusion of the moment and break for their freedom.

The Time Agent was on his feet again. His fury was open and unbridled as he faced the Dominionite officer so that even their companions trembled in their hearts to see it. "How dare you?" he whispered slowly, carefully articulating each word. "How dare you draw against a man who's surrendered to us?"

"That one cut my sire down!"

Murdock forced a rein on his anger. "Your father was a soldier by profession, the commander of Sapphirehold's garrison, and he met his death in open war."

Allran's face flushed with rage. "You mercenaries like to imagine you can civilize war! You cannot, nor have you claim to any cloak of righteousness! We domain people may hire you once in the generation or in several generations when war-need shadows our normally peaceful lifeway, but you yourselves are vampires, ghouls, ever feeding on fresh-spurting blood and dead men's flesh . . ."

Eveleen struck him hard across the mouth. "Shut up, you fool!" The man stiffened but then bowed his head. "Your pardon, Captain. I was grossly insubordinate and accept as merited whatever penalty you lay on me."

"Your anger was better released in shooting off your mouth than in some manner deadly to our honor or our lives. Cool down and then resume your duties."

Ross turned on his heel and walked back toward the Sergeant he had been about to interrogate.

All the captives were staring at him in dazed awe. This man was a legend to them, and they felt in this moment that he was more than any tale or dread could make him. The speed of his response, the strength of his will, his defense of what he held to be justice might momentarily stun them, but all this was only to be expected in the face of what they knew about him. The control he had shown was something different. They had not met with its like before, though these were no recruits having had but little experience with either domain or mercenary officers. They feared him because of it, but they admired him also and held nothing back of their recent history when he put his questions, first to their leader, then to the remainder of them. They had no information that would render such openness a violation of their oaths or a danger to comrades still active in the war.

Murdock came away from the interview disappointed. The Condor Hall men had no news of real interest to him, nor were they couriers, but only the survivors of a larger unit that had been attacked and overcome by partisans farther north. These six had escaped, and since they had already crossed more than half the distance to the front, they had decided that attempting to reach their lines was their wisest course. They had continued southward, hoping that caution and the small size of their party would shield them from further trouble. A careful search had confirmed that they carried no papers or other material useful to the Confederate leaders.

He regretted the delay taking them had cost him. Six warriors, none of them bearing any great rank, made a poor prize. However, they could hardly be released at this point, and Gurnion's people would probably want to examine them more closely in case one or more of them should be carrying secret verbal orders, although that was extremely unlikely. He would not have entrusted any of these with such an errand and did not imagine Zanthor I Yoroc was a poorer judge of men than himself.

Ross was growing uncomfortable about lingering so long and ordered his unit to mount. The prisoners were bound to their springdeer, arms fastened to their sides, and then blindfolded. Soon now, the wild foothills guarding the mountains would be open to them, and they would begin moving south along paths no one not part of Firehand's small army was permitted to see.

They rode hard for some two hours, then halted.

Murdock ordered all eight of his warriors to go with the prisoners, keeping only his three leaders beside him. He and those remaining with him would be at a serious disadvantage if they met with any more of their enemies, but they were near their highlands and were well able to keep themselves concealed until they did reach safety.

The eight soldiers were in less than an excellent situation themselves. They had a goodly distance to go before reaching the Confederate camp, and it would be no delight traveling it in company with prisoners nearly equal in number with themselves.

The Terran would not keep his party intact despite all his awareness of the difficulties separation would and could bring to both units. Luroc, too, must have report of what they had learned in the Funnel. Besides, Murdock never trusted in only one courier or one party to carry news of any importance to their allies. Once he reached his base, more riders would be sent to the Confederate Ton either to confirm the details of his message or to deliver it if these first emissaries had failed to reach him.

22

THE COMMANDER AND his three companions kept moving steadily all that day, trying to regain some of the time they had lost. They were silent for the most part, each busy with his own thoughts, and little was said even when they finally made camp for the night.

Eveleen held the second watch, that following her husband's. She was in no good humor and was glad none of the others was present to see the frown marring her features.

She was furious with Allran. Her fellow Lieutenant was a professional soldier and had honestly acknowledged his fault in addressing his superior as he had, but none of the anger against Murdock which had fired his outburst had faded. He reined it tightly now, but she knew him well enough after their months of service together to be aware of it, and she was certain Ross sensed it as well.

Her expression darkened still further. This was not the first time she had observed discontent or anger on him, either. What was the matter with the man? Ross did not need this with everything else he had to bear besides.

When she was finally relieved, the woman went to where Murdock was lying. Each of the partisans slept apart from his companions, visually separated from them so that some, at least, might escape if their camp were discovered and overrun. She was glad of that now, for it would give them the opportunity for private conversation if her chief were still awake.

Eveleen found Ross lying on his back, his arms pillowing his head. He appeared to be staring into the branches forming the dark roof above him but sat up as soon as she approached.

The Lieutenant gave the signal that all was well and seated herself beside him. "My watch is over," she chided gently. "You should've been asleep ages ago."

"I wanted to do some thinking." He smiled. "You wouldn't have come to me if you didn't expect to find me awake."

"I was afraid you would be," the weapons expert admitted.

"You've got to be played out, too. What's your excuse for staying up?"

Her head lowered and raised again. "The same as yours. I was thinking about what happened today, what Allran said to you."

"He was mad, and he knew I was right."

"Angry words can still wound. He used some pretty strong terms." Her eyes caught his. "Ross, no one, including Allran A Aldar, thinks of you like that."

"Not these people, no. Not now," he said dully, "but all Dominion will soon. You said they shifted into pacifism pretty early. People in our supposed profession wouldn't stay popular in that atmosphere." His eyes fixed on his hands. "I was a misfit in our own time until the Project found me, and I was a misfit in Hawaika's past. Now it's happening again . . ."

"Hardly," she informed him. "The conversion did not happen overnight. Besides, the locals didn't become idiots because they turned away from warfare on a yearly basis. They fought the Baldies, remember, and they did a proper job on them. Their history didn't condemn that stand, or try to drop it into the back of some file and forget it."

A slow smile just touched his lips before fading again. "I suppose I am getting myself worked up over nothing."

His expression darkened again. "I'd have to be stone blind not to see that Allran resents me, though. If he weren't such a professional, there would be serious friction between us even now."

His companion nodded. "It's gotten worse recently. I can't understand what's the matter with him."

"I imagine it's a problem mercenary commanders must occasionally encounter on long-term commissions," Ross said thoughtfully. "Most of these domain leaders are sound warriors and good officers, but their skills are usually confined to training and parading their troops, relieved, perhaps, by bandit control now and then in wilder areas or, in extremely rare instances, by a show of force against some troublesome neighbor.

"When real danger develops, mercenary companies are almost inevitably hired, always with the stipulation that their own officers will have precedence in all war-related activities, save only with respect to the Ton himself."

He sighed. "It's only natural, I suppose, that some of the local men should resent being thus superseded, particularly where rank and birth are interconnected. Such officers simply don't want to yield place to hired swords. I can't say that I blame them."

Ross looked into the distance. "Allran's fathers have commanded Sapphirehold's garrison for five generations. How pleased can I expect him to be to see a mercenary raised over him? Luroc's naming me his son can't have helped, either. It's got to have raised the nasty suspicion that I might stay here and make the current situation permanent. That would be a disaster as far as he was concerned."

The Terran man fell silent a moment, then recalled himself again. "I'll have to do what I can to make peace between us."

"You're not the one at fault!"

"All the same, it's my business to banish this tension before it grows still worse, which it's bound to do if I try to ignore it. We can't afford quarreling in our ranks. That would serve Zanthor so well that it might significantly delay his defeat."

"What more can you do?" Eveleen asked him. "Another man would've decked Allran or worse for what he said to you today."

"I wasn't far from it," her husband confessed.

He shrugged. "All I can do is talk to him. I don't want the place he desires. I should be able to convince him that mercenaries don't stick around once their work's done and life goes back to normal again."

"Will he believe that?"

"He should if I don't hold off so long before speaking to him that his feelings grow permanently irrational. That would be an enormous disservice to an extremely fine officer, and I've delayed nearly too long already."

Ross smiled at her. "That must wait until we're back in base. For now, Lieutenant, I suggest that we both get some sleep. As it is, we won't be happy when it's time to hit the saddle again."

23

THE FOLLOWING DAY dawned pleasantly enough, but the weather turned early in the morning, and soon a sharp, damp wind snapped at them.

Rain joined with it just before noon, a nasty, steady drizzle that kept all four morosely hunched in their cloaks. They were tired in spirit and body after their long mission, they were cold, and even the fact that they were well into the mountains and should reach their base the next day did little to cheer them. None of them felt inclined for speech, although the need for caution was long since past.

All knew camp would be a most unpleasant affair that night, and Murdock weighed continuing on until they reached home.

In the end he decided to break their journey. There was still a goodly distance to go, and he disliked pressing a needless forced march on his companions. He tried never to overtax any of his soldiers without strong cause. They endured quite enough hardship in the normal course of their lives without his adding to their burdens.

The partisans stopped where they were when darkness began to fall despite the fact that the site offered little in the way of comfort. They knew the region in which they traveled and realized they would find nothing better anywhere close by.

At least, they were shielded in great part from the wind. They were in the lee of a high, very sheer cliff that broke the worst of its force. So effective was its screening, in fact, that a considerable amount of soil and softer matter clung to it, bound by the roots of the small, tough plants that had somehow found purchase there despite its almost perpendicular grade.

None of this vegetation was high or very dense, and the rocks and great boulders marbling the cliffside were clearly visible, as were the scars left to show where some of them had torn free.

Ross set their camp a fair distance from the cliff. Falls might not occur frequently, but the stones, some of them large, littering the ground near its base were proof enough that heavy material did occasionally break loose and come down. He was particularly inclined to show caution now. After a day's constant rain, that soil up there was likely to be wet through and maybe somewhat less stable, less able to bear weight against the draw of gravity, than would normally be the case.

A Aldar scowled when he saw where they were to settle. "We would have better shelter closer to the cliff," he protested, "and those two hollows there would let the ones not on watch sleep dry and out of the wind. The bigger of them would hold two of us."

"Some of that rock could too easily fall."

"The ground might tremble and open beneath us, too! If fate wants to take us that way, she will do so, Firehand's precautions be damned!"

The gray eyes turned cold. "Sleep where you will! I've issued no commands on the subject," he snapped, then pointedly turned his attention away from the other.

The Dominionite went to the larger of the two indentations to which he had referred as soon as the usual work of the camp had been completed. His watch did not come until Eveleen's was done, and he could hope for several hours of solid sleep before he was summoned, a considerably better sleep than any of his comrades would enjoy, however weariness might blunt the discomforts of their beds.

Ross could scarcely grip his temper even after he had left the others to take up his turn at guard, and he gave thanks that none of their foes strayed here. With this dark, violent passion so strongly in possession of him, he would have been hard pressed to detect any sort of even minimally subtle approach.

He strove to quell the emotion sending the blood surging through his veins, knowing it to be sharp beyond the affront calling it forth.

The Terran understood well enough why he was reacting like this. The day had been a miserable, tiring one, and he was beginning to feel the backlash of the strain that always accompanied service in the Funnel. A night's proper sleep was what he actually needed to set him right, but until he was free to seek that, he would have to keep himself under very tight check. To his great discredit, he had given way once this night and had no wish to repeat that failing a second time, maybe with even less cause.

A dull rumble tore through the night, followed almost in the same instant by a heart-deadening crash.

The blood drained from the Time Agent's face. He raced for the camp, the certainty of disaster crushing him like a sentence from the judgment chamber of Dominion's Goddess.

It was too well founded. A great stone, a boulder larger than any of the others that had come down before it, had fallen from the cliff to settle against the place where the rebellious Lieutenant had chosen to pass the night. Whether it had broken him beneath its mass or merely trapped him inside could not as yet be determined.

Ross's mouth was a hard line. It could well be that the former was the kinder alternative.

He found no comfort in Gordon's expression when the archeologist turned to give him report. "It's wedged solid. We can't tell whether he's alive, and no air's getting to him if he is. Either we pull him out fast, or we might as well not bother."

His partner nodded grimly. That hole was very small. It would not hold any great supply of oxygen even for one lying prone and inactive, as the prisoner must.

He thought suddenly that it made an excellent tomb.

Murdock gave no voice to that. Allran needed better from him than despair.

He bent to study the boulder and the ground around it.

Bad. Very bad. The land sloped inward toward the cliff, very slightly, perhaps, but still perceptibly, and it was ridged besides so that the great plug was fairly effectively locked in place. It had holed the ground in its striking, too. Fortunately, the latter was itself very hard, and the indentation was slight, but coupled with all the rest and with the weight of the missile, it could too well be enough to defeat them.

He straightened. There was only one real chance that he could see. "Get a couple of the deer. Fasten them to it." He wished they could have used all of the animals, but there was no room for more than a pair of them to maneuver and not enough line to fashion a harness for them even if there were.

His comrades ran to obey.

"You think they'll be able to pull it out?" Eveleen asked doubtfully as she returned with two of their mounts.

"Out, no. They may be able to haul it lengthways along the wall, far enough for us to drag him free."

"A team can't work that way," Ashe told him, "not with the kind of rope harness we'll have to improvise. The path along which they'll have to draw is too narrow. They'd only be pulling against each other."

"We have enough rope to harness them in line, one before the other."

The older man nodded slowly. "Yes," he said softly. "That might just do it."

Working with the speed of desperation, the three soon had the animals readied for the attempt.

The wardeer strained until it seemed that the ropes must surely snap. The stone shivered, moved the barest fraction, then settled back again.

Ross and Gordon threw themselves behind it.

The weapons expert caught Spark's bridle. Fear knotted in her stomach. If that huge thing moved a little space only to roll back again, both men, off balance as they would be, would almost certainly be pinned beneath it.

She called out to the springdeer, and once more, they set themselves against the enormous rock.

Murdock pushed on the stone. His full strength seemed as nothing, but he only forced himself the harder.

He could sense more than see Ashe straining beside him, but he, too, appeared to be powerless . . .

The boulder slipped, edged away from its crater.

Eveleen left her place with the deer. She was beside the men now, waiting, watching.

Inch by agonizing slow inch, it moved, farther and ever farther. How much of the entrance would have to be exposed before the captive—or what remained of him—was free?

The cave opened!

The woman darted inside, caught what she found there, and drew it forth, away from the path the boulder had scraped on the ground.

"He's clear! Jump!"

Both men sprang aside. Ross caught the archeologist's arm to hasten his retreat. The great stone fought the advance it had been forced to make against the slope of the ground, and he doubted the deer would be able to hold it once deprived of the humans' support.

They could not. He saw them begin to slide back themselves and called out a command of release lest the valiant creatures injure themselves in their attempt to remain firm.

He reached them even as he spoke and slashed through their ropes with a quick stroke of his sword.

The rock stood as if frozen for a second's fraction, then rolled back along the scar that marked its passage over the hard ground to strike heavily against the cliffside once more.

The commander did not watch it hit. His comrades were bent over Allran's ominously still form, and he hastened to them.

Eveleen looked up. "He'll be all right. It clipped him when it came down, but he's not much hurt. He should be returning to us shortly."

"Praise Life's Queen for that. . . . I'd best see to the deer. You two, stay with him."

Ross remained a long time with the mounts, which had been pastured several yards away from their riders, and Eveleen at last left her other companions to join him.

"Were they hurt?" she inquired anxiously.

"No, thanks to you and Gordon. You did a good job harnessing them. . . . How's Allran?"

"Well enough. His head's sore, and he's ashamed." Her eyes fixed him. "Why are you avoiding us?"

The man turned away from her. "I don't know how I can face him again. I knew that the danger of this place was real, yet I permitted him to walk straight into it."

"Stop being such an ass!" she snapped irritably. "You were tired and thoroughly miserable. Allran nettled you, and you responded to that. What of it? We're all very well aware already of your fallibility, and it doesn't hurt any of us to have it forced on your own attention now and then."

Her chin lifted as he whirled about. "Blast me for insubordination if you will, but listen and listen good first! If you persist with this nonsense, you'll quite effectively kill any hope of reconciliation with Allran and will probably succeed in ruining him besides. He's certain to read your behavior as your condemnation of him because of his stupidity and fail utterly to recognize it merely as a mark of your own."

Anger flared through Ross, but it quickly cooled. "No man likes to hear that, particularly when it's true."

He took a deep breath, held it, and released it slowly. Feeling calmer now, he forcibly fixed his thoughts on the problem before him. "You're skilled at wagging your tongue, Lieutenant. Do you think Allran would listen to you if you explained to him that I see myself as disgraced by my own part in this affair and ask that he come to me tomorrow after we've reached our camp and have rested a little?"

Her eyes narrowed. "I do if I were willing to abase you. I'm not."

The man smiled. "Peace, Guardian. As you yourself have said, he knows I've been avoiding you tonight. He might as well know why."

"Very well," Eveleen replied, "but there's none of us—especially not Allran—who's going to allow you to accept blame for any of this."

Her tone softened. "You will come back with me now?"

"Yes." Murdock smiled. "Do you imagine I'm going to sulk out here all night and leave the heat of the fire to you three?"

"Who can fathom Firehand's reasoning?" she replied, and then, laughing softly, turned and started back toward their comrades.

It was late afternoon before Allran A Aldar was finally able to bring himself to enter his commander's cabin.

He closed the door quickly behind him to shut out the lashing rain and hung his cloak on the peg fastened to it for that purpose. Water ran from it in small rivers.

Ross looked up from the papers covering his desk. He hoped he did not look as nervous as he felt. This was not the kind of work Ross Murdock did, but it was a commander's business, as much so as was physically fighting the war he was here to wage. He could not delegate it to anyone, not even to Gordon, and he could not weasel out of it. He had only to do it and do it well, for the sake of this young man and for the cause they both supported.

"I was beginning to think I'd have to go looking for you," he said. "Come over here and let the fire drive some of the chill out of you."

The other complied but did not relax despite his chief's easy attitude.

He came to stiff attention before him. "Captain A Murdoc, I realize full well that my conduct at the end of our mission can earn me only contempt. If I had died last night, it should only have been my due."

"Hardly that," Ross replied grimly, "and the loss of your services would certainly not have been the due of the rest of us." Murdock's expression tightened. "Not even mine, although my role was anything but creditable . . ."

"No! Eveleeni told me about that. If the danger had been so obvious, would she or Gordon not have seen it also and have prevented me from exposing myself?"

The commander smiled. "They would, and with that, I think we must close this subject of reproach, both of us. It'll accomplish nothing whatsoever to continue flogging ourselves."

The Lieutenant sat down now. "I wish I knew what has been driving me, setting me against you. I do not will that my temper should ever be so quick to rise."

"You want command of Sapphirehold's garrison and are more than capable of carrying it, and you know I'll remain between you and that authority as long as I stay in Ton I Loran's service."

"I cannot replace Firehand! Even were my vanity as great as one of these mountains, I surely must recognize that!"

"But the war—and with it, the need for my special skills—will soon end, isn't that right?"

Ross leaned forward in his chair. "I'm a mercenary, Comrade. Even after all our time together, you don't realize what that means. I can't stay here. What purpose would I serve? Once Condor Hall is defeated and I see Sapphirehold secure, I'll ride. It's inconceivable that I should do anything else."

His companion was silent a long time. "It speaks ill for my honor, but I concede that you have read me accurately," he responded slowly at the end of that time. "I did not realize this moved me before."

"The reaction's a normal one. Your honor's high enough that it wouldn't permit you to recognize it sooner."

"You believe there is some hope that I shall eventually be given command?"

"I've already recommended that."

Murdock's pale eyes held A Aldar's. "You're a good officer, Allran. You tend to be impetuous, but you're rarely thoughtless and never where those serving beneath you are concerned. You inspire confidence. You're just in your judgments. You plan well in council and respond quickly and appropriately when there's need for sudden change or action."

Ross shrugged. "Waiting even a year or two longer'll be rather to your advantage than otherwise. You're young. Even though our people know your worth, some of the older men could resent serving beneath one so much their junior. The passing of a bit more time will completely lift that potential difficulty from you."

He paused. "Does what I've said sound reasonable to you?"

"Reasonable to my mind. Reasonable to my heart. . . . Rossin, I am sorry. You are too good a friend to Sapphirehold and to me personally for this darkness to have risen up between us."

"Forget it. As Eveleeni feels compelled to remind me, we're only human."

Ross glanced at the papers on his desk with a sigh that was only partly voluntary. "Go on now. I imagine you have scarcely less than this to occupy you, and if you're as beat as I am, you won't be wanting to pass the better part of tonight working at it."

24

THERE WAS LITTLE to mark the following four days. The weather remained extremely ugly with nearly constant, heavy rain accompanied by high winds and, frequently, by sleet.

It cleared a little on the morning of the fifth day, although it was still bitterly cold and the sky remained heavy and leaden.

Ross determined to take a small patrol out despite the threat of more foul weather. He wanted to examine the Corridor for the effect of the recent rains. Parts of it turned to mire after severe, long-term wetting and could become bad enough to prevent the passage of wagons. At this time of year, such conditions, once established, could be expected to hold right to the first snows. If Zanthor I Yoroc wished to move goods then, he would be compelled to use pack animals until the winter put an end to all travel. That would force a significant change in the partisans' work as well; even heavily laden beasts could still move more quickly than vehicles and could traverse a considerably wider range of terrain, although a train of them could not bear nearly as much weight as could a similar number of wagons.

Eveleen was beside Ross. She let her buck shield her from some of the breeze as she tightened his saddle girth.

Ross saw her shiver. "There's no need for you, or Gordon for that matter, to come this time. We don't intend to fight."

"Our abilities no longer satisfy you?" she answered with no good humor.

"I'm only trying to spare you a most unpleasant journey," he told her.

"We always ride with you," she retorted. "When you decide to spare yourself, we'll be spared as well. Until then, we'll hold our prerogatives."

"That's pure stubbornness, Lieutenant."

The woman smiled. "Perhaps I'm only speaking for myself. You might suggest to Gordon that he remain behind."

"I already did. His answer was the same as yours. He just used considerably less restraint in phrasing it."

Ross gave an exaggerated shake of his head. "I won't give any commands. Such folly deserves to reap its full reward."

The Sapphirehold unit rode almost steadily during the next several days. There was a lot of territory to be examined, and the war captain wanted to see it all and be away again as quickly as possible. The Corridor, even this northern part of it, was too close to the invaders' front-line army and was thus too well patrolled to allow him to feel even minimally secure here.

The fact that the invaders tended to send out fairly large units into this region did nothing to comfort him, either. There were only five with him. Their mission was such as to require no more, and it was relatively easy to conceal the movements of so few, yet six was a small number to put against a Condor Hall company.

He sighed then and put a rein on his nervousness. Their purpose was to explore, to study, not to fight. They would send word back to the mountains if they encountered any tempting targets whose capture they might thereby hope to effect, and conceal themselves or flee if they met with a patrol.

His partisans often rode thus and rarely came into trouble because of it. This, he knew full well—had he himself not originated their tactics?—yet the nagging fear of attack, of riding into a trap or a situation they would not be able to handle, continued to plague him unmercifully until he heartily wished they were well away, out of this place and back in the safety of the highlands once more.

Gradually, however, as time passed without difficulty and he gained the information he sought, the Time Agent was forced to congratulate himself for taking the risk of coming here. The rain had indeed done its work. Zanthor of Condor Hall would be sending no wagons through the Corridor for a long time to come.

"We've seen enough," he said at last to the woman riding beside him. "Let's head for home."

His voice had been low. All else was quiet apart from the moaning of the wind, and alien sounds could carry far.

None of the unit was sorry for hearing that order. The endless chill ate at their bodies, and their nerves were raw from trying to keep watch in a country that offered little in the way of defense and no alternate route of escape should they be discovered and need to bolt.

This, then, was what the invaders must feel and endure . . .

The six rode fast and hard, passing at last from the Corridor to the nearly equally dangerous Funnel.

They relaxed somewhat despite the undiminished threat of meeting with a Condor Hall patrol. Here, at least, there was cover, and they had room in which to fight or flee if they did encounter trouble.

The wind was against them, and it was already too late when their springdeer gave them warning. Even as their ears went back, riders rounded the sharply defined bend formed by the base of a low hill just before them, twenty-four of them.

The two parties faced one another, frozen by surprise, only yards apart.

"Through them!" Murdock shouted.

His partisans had learned well the hard lesson of instantaneous response. They charged past their still-stunned foemen.

Their advantage was short-lived. The invaders whirled about and gave chase.

They were close, and their deer, if not fresh, were no more spent than were those of their prey. They would not give up quickly.

Ross dropped back to buy his comrades time. Lady Gay was fast. She would soon bring him away again.

He felled the first rider. The second. Others pressed around him, uncowed by their comrades' deaths. They had recognized him, and knowing his worth to those who could take or slay him, they let their greed fire their courage, greed, and their numbers.

He slashed out, desperately trying to open a path for himself. Two more went down and then a third.

Fire erupted in his side, tore across his stomach.

Murdock slumped forward with a gasp, clutching at Lady's short ridge of mane as the sword dropped from his grasp. The saddle in front of him was already red with his blood.

A shout of triumph began, only to die stillborn.

Others, green-clad warriors, were about him.

The weapons expert's hand steadied him. "Just hang on!"

"Beat it! I'm gutted . . ."

He had no time for more. Someone had Lady Gay's reins and was leading her away.

He glimpsed Eveleen, Gordon, two of the others fighting furiously.

Eveleen? Was she a woman at all or a demoness out of the Halls of Fury?

There was nothing human about this battle. The invaders must have felt the truth of that as well. They buckled, fled, before the unexpected, incredibly fierce counterattack.

After that, there was only the blurred sensation of speed and a constant, jolting agony that seemed somehow unreal, as if it were part of him and yet not part. He clung tightly to Lady but knew he would soon fall were it not for the hands grasping his arms on either side.

At last, the motion stopped. Someone lifted him down. The smith, he thought. Only he could bear a man as if he were a child.

He was placed on the ground, on a cloak. A second was balled and eased under his head.

Marshaling his will, he forced his eyes open, compelled them to focus. "Eveleeni?" His voice was no more than a whisper.

She moved swiftly into his line of sight. "Easy, Rossin. We're away with it."

"All—must not risk themselves—for a dying man. Go on now. This, I—order . . ."

"You are incapacitated, Captain," the woman replied with icy firmness. "I'm in command at the moment."

"Fool . . ."

She placed her fingers over his mouth. "We're not going to give you up, Firehand. I will not."

He had grown too weary for further argument and closed his eyes once more, giving himself over to her will.

His mind retained its awareness. He knew what was happening to him, heard and understood what was being said around him, but it was beyond his power to respond to any of it.

His shirt was torn back and pressure applied to stem what remained of the bleeding. Ashe probed his wound. Ross had felt his touch before in the aftermath of battle and knew it now.

Gordon's breath caught. "The Lord of Time be praised," he whispered, his voice oddly thick. "I don't think the intestines have been cut."

He demanded water, which soon came. It was hot, and Ross moaned.

Eveleen's fingers gently caressed his forehead and temple. "Hold on, Love. It'll be over soon."

"I wish we could chance a duller," a man's voice, the blacksmith's said; there was an anguish in it that surprised him.

They would give him no pain killer, of course. Gordon had no more of the supply issued him at their mission's outset, and Murdock's body could not tolerate the local substance. If he sickened now, with such a wound, he was dead.

Ashe probed the laceration again, this time cleaning as well as examining. "I'm nearly certain they're sound, but it was a close miss, and he's by no means free of danger. He can't take any more tearing. . . . I'll need help with the bandages. They'll have to be tight."

Ross felt another touch him, one of the men. The binding process was harsh. He lost consciousness during part of it, and when he drifted back into semiawareness, his mind was too confused to make an identification.

He heard Eveleen order someone to ride for the mountains, and then blackness closed in over him.

The war captain shivered violently. Someone was holding a frigid cloth to his face.

He tossed his head to rid himself of the tormenting thing and opened his eyes.

Gordon was beside him. He looked tired and strained, and there was an open fear on him which he now strove to conceal.

"How are we doing?" Ross was pleased that his voice, though weak, was at least steady. It sounded strange to his ears, as if he heard it through some kind of aural fog.

"Quite well. We're just ending a short break now. By riding through the night, we should be home by this time tomorrow."

"Any sign of the invaders?"

"None."

"My wound?" he asked after a brief pause.

"Bad enough," Ashe answered evenly, "but not so serious as we first supposed. You've got a high fever, and that could prove more dangerous to you than your actual injuries if it gets much worse."

"I'm able to ride now, at least slowly. Let me have Lady. I can make my way back at my own pace . . ."

Gordon's eyes flashed in sudden fury, but then he laughed. "You read too many adventure novels back home, Friend. We're not going to let you ride off to a solitary death in sacrifice for us all. Besides, that's not necessary."

Murdock sighed, knowing there would be no moving his partner.

He had to try. "Gordon, some of those men escaped. They

recognized me, and they'll soon spread the word that Firehand has been seriously wounded and must still be within their power of taking. Half Condor Hall's army'll be out in force after us if they aren't already."

Eveleen joined the pair at that point. She sat beside them. "Hunting and capturing are two different matters," she informed him in a tone that brooked no argument.

He nodded, as if in defeat. "At least, you might give me something to ease the pain.

The woman laughed then and bent to kiss him. "So you can force your own body into slaying you? I think not, Firehand. Anyway, I doubt it would work. I don't believe your injuries are that severe, especially since they haven't worsened under the motion of the litter. You'd only succeed in making yourself dreadfully sick."

"You can't make any speed while I'm with you!" he argued desperately. "I know enough of wounds to realize that. Am I to see you all killed, to be the cause of it?"

Ashe smiled down on him. "Not a chance. We're as safe now, or nearly as safe, as if we were in the midst of our own camp. Listen to the noise of the deer around us! We're with a goodly company. Scouts are combing all the country about to carry warning if the enemy should approach, and skirmish patrols are riding near on every side to challenge and delay any who might be so foolish as to appear.

"Condor Hall-born warriors may be famed for fighting with a fanatic's zeal, but all their fury is nothing to that which we're prepared to show now. We'll defend our own, my Friend. Believe that, and rest easy."

"It might all be for nothing," he whispered, reassured almost despite himself.

"Then you'll at least die at home, with whatever comfort we can provide for you," Eveleen told him quietly.

As she had done to silence him before, she pressed her fingers to his lips. "Shut up now, and don't let me hear any more talk about dying. I'm not about to surrender you, Firehand, not even to that grim Lord."

Ross was conscious of a strange, swaying movement, its rhythm occasionally broken by unpredictable jerks or drops that wrung a moan or a cry of protest from him, however the weak control he still possessed over his body tried to quell it.

At times, he would be puzzled or totally disoriented but then would force himself to concentrate.

He rode in a deer litter. It was not the first time he had traveled thus, but on that other occasion, he had been able to fix himself to his position, consider his unit's needs. Now, it was hard to focus his thoughts at all, impossible to hold them any length of time . . .

It was cold, bitterly cold. Not all these blankets they had piled on him seemed able to hold it away from him, as if it originated within his own flesh rather than in the sleet now lashing down in a continuous storm.

Once, maybe twice, he thought he felt heat. There was far too much of it. His body poured sweat, and he struggled against the weight of his coverings until powerful arms restrained him.

Those warm spells, if he had not dreamed them entirely, did not last long, and he was more than glad to feel the end of them and have the cold sweep back over him once more.

Gradually, the troubling episodes came less frequently. A deep oblivion rose up to take him, and he drifted down into it, secure at last from discomfort and from the sharp talons of pain.

25

THE TIME AGENT lay perfectly still. His body was at ease. There was no motion, no movement at all. He was resting on a comfortable bed. Pillows supported him at an angle steeper than that at which he was wont to sleep, a measure to help keep his lungs clear. The air around him was wonderfully warm.

A muted light reached his lid-veiled eyes. It teased him, and in the end, he opened them.

He frowned. This was not his chamber.

"So you wake at last!"

He turned his head.

. Luroc was sitting beside him. The Ton moved swiftly to adjust the pillows so that the injured man might sit higher. "Easy. You are in my cabin."

"Why?" he asked.

"It is the warmest and most comfortable in the camp. . . . You had us all very worried this last week, Rossin."

"A week? So long?"

He nodded. "Yes. Until the fever left you this morning, we were in doubt as to whether you would live."

A strangely strong sense of loss filled him when he suddenly realized that neither Eveleen nor Gordon was present.

I Loran seemed to read his thought. "I just sent your comrades to get some rest. Between commanding our war effort and nursing our illustrious wounded, they are both about spent."

The ruler chuckled. "Do not scowl so! You cannot expect everything to hold still because you have been put out of it for a time. As a matter of fact, those hunting you have provided our people with some excellent targets."

"They shouldn't have wasted themselves here . . ."

"You could have kept away had one of them been hurt, I suppose?"

Murdock was visibly growing tired, and I Loran pushed his chair back, away from the bed. "No more for now. It is near midnight. Eveleeni will see you tomorrow and will give you as full a report as Healer O Ashean declares you are able to hear. In the meantime, you are to rest. We all fought a hard battle to save you, and I am not about to risk setting you back again by overtaxing you."

Recovery did not come quickly. The wound itself closed in good order, but the fever returned twice more, each time stripping away whatever the war captain had regained of strength, and the winter was well spent before he had at last been permitted to return to his own quarters.

In truth, he had not pressed to leave the Ton's cabin. It was warm there, and he seemed no longer able to tolerate cold. Any cold. Even now, long after the other effects of the wound had begun to vanish, he could still bear no touch of chill. So severe was his reaction against it that unless it lessened again with the passage of time, significantly lessened, Ross feared he would be forced to limit his long-term activities either to the far south here or to hot paradise worlds like Hawaika, venturing into other climates only for short, summer assignments.

Murdock put that thought from him. He had to trust that this blight would eventually leave him as the fever had finally done. In the meantime, he could only endure it as best he might, that and conceal his continuing discomfort from his companions.

Save in this one respect, he had reason in plenty to be pleased. His own strong constitution had reasserted itself, and he had regained both the flesh he had lost and his wonted energy, which had so far deserted him that he had for the most part been content to remain docile under his attendants' commands.

Not, the Terran thought with a grin, that protest would have done him much good. His comrades had been determined that he should be fully whole again before resuming command over his troops, and no amount of impatience on his part would have turned them from that.

By all Time's levels, though, it was good to feel well and ready to take up his life once more. For a while there, after the second return of the fever, he had thought no future remained to him but that of an invalid.

He put that fear, which had been bitterly strong in its time, out of his mind, as well. It was an unpleasant memory, but at least it had failed to materialize into fact.

He had not even missed a great deal of actual fighting. If his blade had remained long months in its scabbard, so had those of his comrades. There had been raiding in the three weeks following his wounding, but then the winter had settled down in its full fury. It had been a bad one, as the signs had indicated would be the case, with heavy snow and week upon week of brutally low temperatures. Nothing had moved either on the slopes or in the lowlands.

The coming of spring ended that enforced truce.

As soon as the Corridor became passable again, the invaders started pushing materiel south, and the Sapphireholders swept down from their eyrie to counter them. Murdock had led four of those raids with such effect that, whatever Zanthor I Yoroc might wish or will to the contrary, both Confederates and the invader's own warriors knew Firehand was neither dead nor frightened from his work, and some doubted that he had ever been stricken down at all.

The war captain broke from his reverie. A springdeer had just come into the camp, galloping hard.

Perhaps he only imagined it, but he always thought there was a certain sound in the hoofbeats of a mount whose rider brought word of a potential target not present at other times, and that elusive note seemed to ring from these.

Ross did not wait for the courier to draw rein before his cabin, but crossed that part of the floor separating him from the door in three swift strides. He threw it open.

A scout, right enough. Marri.

The woman was just dismounting when he reached her.

"You have news?" It was hardly necessary to inquire. The still sharp air might have brought the red to her cheeks, but the excitement in eye and expression did not arise out of any such cause.

"I do, Captain. Deermen, a large column of them."

"Pack train?"

She shook her head. "No. They have drays with them, but only enough to carry supplies for maybe a couple of weeks."

"Going south?"

"They were, and traveling fast."

"You say the column is long?"

"One hundred warriors plus officers."

He pursed his lips. "They could as easily divide, remain in the lowlands to harry us."

"I doubt that is their intent, Captain. Their composition is strange, apparently very heavy with officers. That is why I spoke of them separately from the others."

"Apparently?"

"Cover was not good. We dared not draw too close to them."

Ross glanced at his chief Lieutenant, who was standing beside him along with the rest of his officers. "Command change for the front maybe?"

"Possibly," she agreed. "Very possibly. Zanthor must be getting itchy for victory again. He's known little of it since the first year."

Murdock turned back to the scout. "Were the warriors mercenaries, Marri, or his own?"

"Condor Hall men to the last, and fine looking even for those from what we could tell."

He thanked her, then turned to those with him. "Eveleeni's division and mine ride. Allran, head for the Corridor. I want to be sure nothing's slipped through if this is just a lure. Korvin, strengthen the passes. It's not likely, but I can't risk that one of them may be their target. The rest of you, stay here. Keep yourselves ready to ride if you should receive summons from any of us, leaving a double guard with the camp. Have couriers ready to bring word at once if anything else develops."

Allran A Aldar frowned at these orders. "It is a big column. Perhaps you should bring another division with you."

"I'll play it as it comes. If necessary, I'll call for help, but I can't afford to leave ourselves open to any smart moves on Zanthor's part. He knows better than we do that he's nearing the end of his strength. If he's going to pull his cause out of the fire, he's got to do it now. We'll have to be able to meet any plot he hatches, or we could lose a lot of ground." For a moment, his voice turned bleak. "Maybe we could lose the whole lot."

26

THE PARTISANS RODE hard, following the line Marri had told them any additional couriers would take. So mobile a target, one whose purpose was unknown, could change its course at any moment.

The enemy column kept to its original path, holding to the center of the lowlands as far as possible from the flanking mountains, always maintaining as rapid a pace as possible without exhausting their mounts.

Although gentler than the great peaks themselves, the countryside thorugh which they traveled was rough enough in its own right and grew even more so as the lowlands narrowed into the Funnel. Cover was good, and the partisan leaders were at last able to move in close to their foes.

It was an impressive company by any standards. There was a military perfection to the warriors' movements not often found in domain-based units, and they bore themselves and their arms with the quiet assurance of proven veterans.

There was pride in them, too. These were the men who had made Zanthor's early conquests, forging for him an empire strong enough to enable him to maintain the mercenary columns now carrying his war. It was no fault of theirs that these same hirelings had failed to hold the momentum they had established.

Murdock's attention fixed on the officers.

His eyes narrowed. Marri had been right. The column was top-heavy with them.

If they were its commanders, they were its charge as well; they rode in the center, protected by the warriors all around them, and that lot were no cowards, whatever their other failings.

The majority of the invading domain's leaders were known to the partisans and he concentrated on identifying those before him. The men chosen to carry this mission might well give a clue to its purpose, although he felt fairly certain now that they were to either change or strengthen the command structure of the army in the south.

That was a daring move to make when dealing with mercenaries, who could be volatile in the extreme in the face of any threat to their position or prerogatives, but it had been done before, sometimes with good result. As long as contracted payments were made in due time, the Ton of Condor Hall might well succeed in accomplishing his will.

That thought caused the agent's frown to deepen. Troops so led could prove far more formidable opponents than Gurnion's commanders were now expecting to meet.

He stiffened. One caught his gaze, a broad-shouldered man, thick of neck with very dark, slightly curling hair—he bore his helm in his hand—and the dark shadow of a beard on his face although the day was still comparatively young.

Zanthor I Yoroc.

A curse, whispered but bitter, sounded on his left. No word, not so much as the drawing of a breath, issued from the woman holding the place at his right.

Ross glanced at her, and the heart chilled within him. Eveleen Riordan stood perfectly still, more like a marvelous statue than a living being. Her gaze was fixed on the would-be conqueror, and never had he imagined that hatred of this intensity could exist in any member of his species, in any being fashioned by the hand of the Great Creator.

It did not mar her as he knew he had been marred a moment before. No line of her face was altered by it, yet it burned through her, emanated from her, terrible beyond all conception in its controlled stillness. If the will of a Terran could slay, Zanthor of Condor Hall would be crumbling to ashes in this moment.

Ross gave the signal to withdraw, and the five partisans silently moved back, away from the rapidly advancing column.

They were not long in reaching their comrades. The news that the invader Ton was near and within their potential grasp brought a low growl of mingled rage and exultation from the assembled warriors, but their commander would allow no move against Zanthor, not yet.

It was Ross's intention to strike his enemies just as they were forming their evening's camp, when the most men were dismounted and least prepared for combat and the guards, if out at all, would not be fully settled into their watching. He had not forgotten the prowess of Condor Hall soldiers or what it had cost his own command in their last encounter.

It was not just his people that he wanted to spare, either. By coming at Zanthor's warriors as he intended, more of them could probably be felled with less-than-fatal strokes than would be the case if they were attacked as the alert, battle-ready unit the column had revealed itself to be. Murdock had no more love than did Gurnion I Carlroc for the needless slaughter of valiant men.

The Sapphirehold partisans timed their arrival carefully so that their charge could begin at the moment their chief had indicated.

Ross's mouth was a hard line. The attack would not be quite as effective as he had originally hoped. The Condor Hall commander had not so settled his force as to render it easy for the taking. His position was high although well sheltered, readily defensible, and holding the surrounding area under its view. If the partisans were able to strike as planned and do so quickly, they should still be able to conquer. If the charge were delayed or if their presence came somehow to be suspected before it began, they would be forced to storm the enemy position as if it were a fort, or else to retreat.

It would be the latter, whatever their eagerness to take Zanthor. Sapphirehold did not have the troops to squander in costly frontal

assaults. Harrying tactics had served them well through all this
campaign and would serve them here if needs be until they could
find a position from which to attack again in force. With luck, one
of the archers might be able to pick I Yoroc off from ambush even
if they were unable to join open battle.

The war captain turned in his saddle to look upon his own
warriors, studying them so intently for several seconds that they
felt his scrutiny and glanced toward him in both amazement and
discomfort.

He had to be certain their hate was in control. If it were not, it
could betray them all.

His head raised. He wronged them. These domain soldiers were
no less than the professionals hired by Gurnion I Carlroc or those
manning the Project at home. Calm was demanded of them now,
and this they would give, whatever their feelings against the ruler
of Condor Hall.

His heart was beating hard and fast. The battle ahead of them
could be the ending or the final turning of the war. If they could
fell or take Zanthor . . .

His comrades would be no less aware than he of what their
efforts could bring, to their domain and island if not to Dominion
of Virgin herself. Scant wonder they stood beside him in this icy,
almost stunned stillness.

He drew a deep breath to steady himself and then straightened.
The invaders would be no more vulnerable than they were at this
moment.

Almost in slow motion, the Terran raised his battle horn to his
lips and sounded the command to charge.

Ross Murdock had fought many times and in many different ways
during his life but rarely before in a battle that equaled this either
in fury or in the skill and determination, the raw courage, of the
participants.

The Condor Hall men, warriors and officers alike, yielded no
inch of ground not soaked red with their own and their enemies'

blood, nor did their efforts lessen when it at last became evident that the partisans would gain the day.

Ross's skill was heavily tried. It was the officers that he sought out, knowing their fall was damning not only to their comrades here present but to the invaders' cause as a whole, and as was the case with his own command, many of them appeared to have won rank with courage and ability rather than through mere favor or birth. They did not go down readily, and not all those falling did so without setting their mark on him so that his clothing was rent and red-stained in several places by the time his soldiers began to bring the confrontation to a close.

He ignored the wounds. None was of any significance, and with the battle-fire on him, he scarcely felt them. Soreness would come later, when quiet returned to his mind and body. For now, unless they began to stiffen prematurely and thus slowed his movements, they were of no interest to him.

Zanthor, too, had felt the bite of his enemies' weapons and bore their tears even as did his foeman. Like the Terran Captain's, his sword was brilliantly wielded, brilliantly and with deadly accuracy. None who faced him stood long against him.

Always, the two commanders sought to join combat, and always, the press of the fighting kept them apart. At last, however, each found himself free of opponents and with a clear path open between them.

Murdock set himself to charge, but another rider bore suddenly down upon the invader, and he drew his doe aside. "For your people," he whispered. Dread was a knife twisting in his heart, but he knew if he refused Eveleen Riordan this right, it would stand between them for whatever remained to either of them of life.

The Ton of Condor Hall saw him pull back and stared at him a moment in amazement. He well knew that this accursed partisan did not fear to confront him.

Zanthor saw the one who was to challenge him then and laughed. Did this sharp-faced slip of a girl actually imagine she could match blades with him, however adept she was at lurking in shadows?

It was almost a pity, he thought as he spurred his springdeer toward her. He would have enjoyed breaking her in another way.

Their swords met, slid off one another, and met again.

The man's amusement vanished. EA Riordan was good, very good, even as her reputation declared her to be, and she fought in the odd fashion of these Sapphireholders so that his bulk and his longer reach gave him no advantage over her.

That might alter if he could wear her down, weary her.

It was no use. The wench kept him moving, denying him any chance to spare himself for later assault.

The contest went on. He himself was tiring, and still he could find no weakening in her guard, nothing upon which he could capitalize. Her light blade danced maddeningly before his eyes, seemingly without effort on her part, certainly without flaw. There appeared to be no pattern upon which he could fix, nothing he could prepare to meet or counter . . .

The woman's sword spun into a small circle, daintily striking aside his own heavy weapon and darting forward in one liquid motion. Its point pierced his left eye and the brain behind it.

27

MURDOCK LOOKED UP at the man standing between two of his partisans. The prisoner was young, approximately the same age Ross had been when he had joined the Project. He was slight, almost twisted, of body, but he bore himself proudly, hardly surprising given the officer's stripe on his battle-stained uniform and the cast of his features, which the broad bandage encircling his head could not conceal.

Tarlroc I Zanthor. Two other sons of the slain Ton had perished in the fight, but this one had been felled by a blow to the skull and taken still breathing.

The partisan leader had been aware of his capture since the battle's end, but there had been a great deal to be done—arranging the care of the wounded, sending out patrols and sentries to guard against a counterattack, starting a systematic search of the Condor Hall camp—and that had claimed his first attention. Besides, he had wanted to have both Gordon and Eveleen present at this interview, which would not have been possible any sooner.

Loud voices, sharp with hate, were audible outside the tent in which the Sapphirehold leaders sat. Now that everything immediately possible had been done for the living, the dead were being gathered for burial. To judge by the present commotion, I Yoroc's corpse must have just been drawn up from the slope.

Tarlroc read the meaning of the sounds as well. For an instant, his control threatened to shatter, but he was practiced in holding a rein on himself, and he kept his face and stance impassive before his captors.

Ross observed the quickly masked quiver of emotion pass over the younger man. He could pity the sudden loss of a father and brothers without regretting the deaths themselves. "Tell them to keep it quiet out there," he ordered the two guards. "Just take care of the dead, theirs and ours, and get the wounded ready to move."

Once the pair left to obey, he turned to his prisoner. "Your kin will be buried with the rest of your fallen, as is necessary to prevent the spread of sickness. No dishonor will be shown them. As for yourself, I want some answers from you."

"You cannot expect me to provide them," I Zanthor responded quietly, with a dignity that belied his youth. "Even if I had them," he added with carefully schooled bitterness. "My father always kept his plans to himself until he was ready to act. Even the Ton-heir might not have been informed of his purpose."

Would they believe him? They might, for Zanthor had always been known to play his game close, long before he had started on the road to domination. And death.

As for himself, Tarlroc I Zanthor was a minor light, a clerk, not a warrior at all unless unavoidably pressed by circumstances as in this last, tragic battle.

Condor Hall was lost anyway, he thought dully, whether he held quiet or not. Neither the new Ton nor his other surviving brother was a man to equal Zanthor I Yoroc. They would not be able to hold the war effort together much less carry out the rape of the south, even in the unlikely event that their sire had communicated his intentions to one or the other of them. One of the mercenary commandants might possibly be able to do so, functioning behind a figurehead Ton, but none of the three was clearly dominant now, and he could not see any of them seizing control in time to accomplish any good.

Maybe they had been fated to fail in any case. In that event, Zanthor was fortunate to have fallen here, albeit at the hand of an ugly woman scarcely bigger than a child, rather than later and far more slowly to the so-called justice of his enemies.

A sudden surge of loss and hate filled him. "It is the demons who should have died," he whispered through set lips. "They encouraged Zanthor to begin the war and then withheld the aid that would have given him victory."

A strangling dread crushed Murdock's heart, but his brows only raised. "Are you trying to excuse Zanthor, to say that he was one who obeyed voices sounding in the air around him?"

"Zanthor I Yoroc bowed to no one's will, and the only voices he heard came from throats solid enough to grasp and strangle."

"Go on." The Condor Hall man said nothing more, and Ross Murdock leaned forward. "You claim these supposed allies betrayed Zanthor, at least to the extent of refusing significant help. Tell us what happened. It is the only way you have left of avenging him."

I Zanthor studied Firehand. He was determined not to compromise his sire's cause or his brothers' efforts, however futile, but the big heads were no part of Condor Hall's war. They had no claim on his loyalty.

The partisan leaders were silent for some moments after he had finished his tale. At last, Murdock called for the guards, who had been waiting outside the tent. "Watch him carefully," he commanded, "and see that nothing happens to him. We may want to question him again."

His eyes closed as the Dominionites left the tent. "Baldies," he whispered.

"They're well met." Eveleen Riordan shivered. "That man frightens me more than they do."

Her eyes flashed in anger. "His father was betrayed! There's no word about his father's neighbors or the women and babies butchered or those dying in battle, for and against Condor Hall!"

"Terra knows his kind all too well," Ashe said grimly. "Psychiatrists . . ."

"Damn it, Gordon, don't go bleeding heart on me!" Ross snapped. "Tarlroc I Zanthor and his old man weren't little lambs led into evil ways by the big, bad Baldies. They knew full well what they were doing, and they went right ahead and did it."

"Precisely. So do the people I was describing. Psychopaths, sociopaths, antisocial personalities—call them what you will, they're sane, they're aware of the harm they do, and they simply do not care. Nearly all our serial killers have been of that breed and most of the real military and political monsters as well."

The other man's eyes dropped. "I'm sorry, Gordon, but what are we going to do, or how are we going to do it, rather? On Hawaika, we had the Foanna's magic, and we were still nearly whipped. Here, all we have are swords and bows to set against everything those devils can command."

The archeologist shook his head. "They're tough, but don't make the mistake of believing them more formidable than they are." He smiled at the incredulity in his comrades' expressions. "First off, we won't be facing anything like we did on Hawaika. The Baldies themselves had tapped into on-world powers there. That's what created most of the havoc. There were a lot more of them as well. Here, we have only five . . ."

"That's all I Zanthor saw at a given time," Eveleen interjected. "I'd bet a month's pay that he can't tell one Baldy from another any more than we can."

"Good point," Murdock agreed, "but I think Gordon's right on that point. This seems to be a small party sent to get Zanthor to do their killing for them." His lips tightened as bitter memories rose in his mind. "Five of them are more than enough of a challenge."

"A challenge we can reduce," Ashe told him. "We know from your own experience and also from I Zanthor's that they can be surprised, and they cannot wield their mental powers as long as they themselves are physically occupied. I stayed conscious during that battle on Hawaika longer than you did, long enough to be certain of that. We'll have to hit them fast and hard so they don't have a chance to bring their mental or physical weaponry into play, but it is at least theoretically possible for us to take them."

Ross scowled at his partner. "There's a problem with theory. It doesn't always work out in practice."

The other smiled. "It's up to us to make it work."

The partisan commander nodded, deadly serious now. "The attack party will have to be small, limited to ourselves probably, and we'll have to go in deerless on the last leg of the approach. That was how Zanthor and Tarlroc managed to surprise them. If we can't gain that edge, we might as well just pack up and go home. Our Baldy friends'll either burn us down or immobilize us before we ever reach their camp."

"If they're still there," Eveleen said.

"No reason why they shouldn't be." He frowned. "That's one point that really puzzles me. Why have they just sat it all out for so long? Those boys aren't shy, or at least, they've taken active roles everywhere else that we've encountered them. Why are they so passive here?"

"I'd like to know why—or how—they're here at all," Gordon Ashe remarked. "This is more than seven centuries ahead of their time."

That observation gave his companions a nasty jolt. Ross licked his lips. "It's how many millennia ahead of ours? . . . Time travel?"

"They're nothing if not technologically sophisticated, and they did get a good look at our rivals' setup back on Terra."

"Then no place, no era, is safe from them . . ."

"Let's stop raising windmills to fight, shall we?" Eveleen told her comrades. "There are a number of possible explanations for the Baldies' presence here and now besides the one that brought us. For one thing, we ran into them at a certain stage in their history. They had to be around a lot longer than that and be star traveling longer. These could be discoverers or a team sent to seed long-term trouble."

Ashe nodded. "That makes sense. They're trying to keep a low profile."

"Maybe they just can't do more," Murdock suggested. "By the sound of it, they've had equipment problems on a major scale almost from the start. They must have managed to reach Dominion, or part of the intended team did, brought their camp gear, supplies, and the gold with them, but they couldn't get the rest. They have to be short to be using their lasers for repair tools."

"Not to mention trying to patch things up with native metals and maybe trying to manufacture the components they need out of them as well," Gordon agreed.

"Beggars usually have to take what they get, whether they plead for alms or demand them," Eveleen remarked.

"Zanthor I Yoroc would have been a singularly ungenerous donor. He may well have doomed his own cause by his tightness. Even Baldies couldn't fight if they didn't have the means."

"He might also have preserved his own hide, from them at least. They'd have been quick to eliminate him once he had done the job they wanted, especially since both he and his son were resistant to mental control."

The Lieutenant pushed her chair away from the rough table and stood up. "We might get a few answers when we check out their camp, assuming we survive the attempt to take it. . . . Do you think I Zanthor will cooperate enough to guide us there?"

"He'll cooperate," her husband said, "that far anyway. He apparently did love his father, and he suffered considerable abuse from those devils himself. We represent his only chance to get a crack at them."

"Unless he's spun us a fine story," she suggested darkly.

"That's hardly impossible, but he'll still lead us to them, to our sorrow if we can't outwit the lot of them. We can be sure of one thing. Tarlroc I Zanthor did encounter Baldies. He's right on too many points for him to be faking that."

28

THE PARTISAN COMMANDER eased his way past a thick stand of brush crowding the narrow path. This was it, the culmination of two weeks made hellish by ever-growing dread and the anticipation of disaster.

It was fitting, he supposed, Terran Time Agents once again directly confronting the Baldies whose drive for destruction they were attempting to thwart. The only trouble was that they stood too good a chance of losing. Losing their lives and more than their lives. Losing Dominion of Virgin.

Tarlroc I Zanthor, who had been walking a few paces ahead, stopped and waited for him. "Let me have a knife if not a sword."

"Just stay out of it when the trouble starts, if it does."

"You will not trust me?"

"Would you trust us?"

The Dominionite's eyes narrowed. "You may not be talking so proudly soon, Firehand," he snarled, "or talking at all. Those we brought with us the first time never spoke again. The demons made statues of them."

"We shall see how they fare with us, if your demons are there at all."

That response was required by the role he played, but Ross Murdock felt better for having voiced it. He had confronted these foes before, and each time, he had come away unbroken. He could hold that knowledge as an inner shield, a brace for his courage, in whatever was all too soon to come.

A new surge of fear set his heart racing. It was almost time. They had picketed their springdeer half a mile back. An hour's walk at this cautious pace would bring them to the starmen's camp.

His hands balled despite his effort to keep them open at his sides. Lord of Time, was it this bad for Eveleen and Gordon as well? Could it be? They had never stood alone on a windswept beach and faced down that raw will to conquer . . .

Ross's heart was still hammering, but his mind and emotions were under tight control. They had to be. He was crouching at the edge of the clearing Tarlroc had described, and his targets were before him.

Four targets. The fifth Baldy was not in sight. Bad. That boded trouble for later, but there was no help for it. They must strike at once or lose the power of surprise that was their only hope of victory.

The Time Agent's hand raised in signal to his comrades. As it did, their bows released, and two of the spacers fell.

Murdock lifted his own weapon to set an arrow to it. He struggled to draw, but it was as if he were battling an atmosphere suddenly turned to molasses. He willed himself to continue, but his hands were shaking so badly that he could not aim.

Will? The Baldies, damn them! The two survivors were using their powers of mind to immobilize their attackers. He could feel the tugging at his mind, the weighting of his limbs. He could still move despite the force of their command—perhaps his previous exposures had sharpened his resistance—but he lacked the coordination to shoot effectively.

He groaned as the starmen changed their method of attack and pain exploded in his head. Ross knew this agony. He set himself to fight it as he had fought that day on Terra's Bronze Age beach.

It was even more urgent that he conquer this time. He could sense, feel, a difference in purpose in his opponents. Before, they had wanted to take him. Now they intended to burn his mind away.

His comrades were under the same pressure. He heard a moan from Gordon, a little whimper from Eveleen, but he could give them no help. He was losing this one himself . . .

The Baldies felt their victory and increased the power of their assault. Murdock was helpless now. His will was still holding, but he could channel none of it to his body.

"No, you don't," Eveleen Riordan hissed suddenly. Her voice was low and hoarse but clearly audible to him. "Not to me, you don't."

All at once, the pressure on him vanished. The Time Agent blinked in surprise, then fixed his eyes on those in the clearing. To his amazement, one of the Baldies was clasping his head as if in agony. The other had ceased to attack; his thoughts were coiled in a protective barrier around him.

Murdock's breath caught. He recalled what the Foanna had said about Eveleen's defenses, that she, too, had mental shields but that she inflicted more pain than he did in her refusal to admit them. The weapons expert had only been guarding herself against the too-close advance of those she knew to be friends. Here, with real anger, fear, and hate to drive her, she was fighting an active battle.

She could not hold two such opponents indefinitely. Even as he watched, the less affected of the pair reached for the slender rod hooked to his belt.

Ross let fly an arrow. It missed but startled the other long enough for Murdock to slam into him, throwing him to the ground.

The spacer struck him sharply in the chest, hard enough to wring a grunt out of him. Had that blow caught him in the throat as intended, Murdock would have been out of the fight before it had half started.

Ross was prepared for a stiff battle. He had learned in that first encounter years before that these aliens were tough and strong despite their thin, seemingly frail bodies.

The Baldy had already half drawn his laser and was now trying to bring it to bear. Murdock's hand clamped over the other's, twisting desperately in his effort to keep the business end turned away from him.

A crackling hiss and streak of vicious light and heat drove Ross back, forcing him to release his hold. He braced himself for the death that now seemed inevitable, but his opponent had fallen as well and lay still. The agent saw why. Half the face had been burned away and all that part of the skull and brain above it.

Murdock wasted no time. He whirled in response to the sounds of a second struggle.

Gordon Ashe and the remaining Baldy were locked in one another's grasp, each striving to secure a solid grip on the other's throat.

The spacer was not ignorant of the ways of unarmed combat and had the wiry strength of his kind, but he customarily fought with mind and weapons that killed from a distance. The Terran had trained long and hard in the various methods of close combat for his previous missions and for this one. That experience was giving him an edge now.

It ended abruptly. Ashe gained the hold he sought. There was a strange, sharp crack, and the Baldy's large-domed head lolled to one side with a grotesque freedom that proclaimed the spinal column was broken.

The archeologist remained where he was, breathing heavily. Murdock reached him in a moment. "Gordon?" he asked anxiously.

The other looked up. "I'm all right." He came to his feet, then turned to seek their companions.

Eveleen Riordan had emerged from the cover surrounding the clearing, bringing their ashen-faced prisoner with her. She herself was starkly white, her face a strained mask, but she knelt at once beside the nearest of the aliens, then straightened and moved to the next.

She stiffened. "Rossin! Gordon! This one's alive!"

Both men hurried over to her. She glanced up at them. "I don't think he'll hold on much longer."

Ashe nodded grimly. The arrow, Gordon's own, which had felled the spacer, protruded from his chest. It had been well placed and had penetrated deeply. Blood, or the Baldy's equivalent, bubbled on his lips. It was red, logical enough in an oxygen-breathing being, the archeologist supposed, but something more exotic would have seemed more appropriate, a green or black fluid, or perhaps a colorless ichor.

While he was noting these details and his patient's labored breathing, he worked to free the unfamiliar fastenings holding the tunic closed prior to attempting to cut away the incredibly tough material.

The Baldy's eyes opened. They focused for a moment. There was no anger in them or in the weak emotion field the dying starman broadcast, no fear or hate or bitterness, just contempt, one vast sea of it. The eyes dulled then, and the last ragged effort to breathe shuddered to a stop.

29

ROSS'S FINGERS CLOSED gently on Eveleen's arm. "Thanks." She only nodded numbly, and his grip tightened. "Did they hurt you?"

The woman took hold of herself. "No, not permanently, just while it was going on."

"What happened? What did you do?"

"I don't know, not to be able to explain it." She paused, then went on, choosing her words carefully. "I knew what those bastards were trying to do, of course, and I was terrified. Then suddenly, I got red, flaming mad and just fought back. When I realized I had not only eased the pressure on us but was actually getting to them, I kept it up. They drove me back fast, but I'd held out long enough to buy you and Gordon time to jump back into the war."

That they had won was still a near miracle, Murdock thought. Eveleen had given them their opening, but luck had been with them, or, rather, a weakness of the Baldies themselves had been, a weakness his kind might be able to exploit again. The spacers apparently drew upon their mental abilities as their weapons of choice. Had they gone for their lasers first, the story would probably have had a different end. Of a certainty, all four humans would not be in one piece at this point. The noble barbarian generally did not fare well when trying to set his sword and bow against the arms of a vastly technologically superior foe.

Ross bent over the spacer's body and unfastened the loaded

utility belt, which he carefully worked free of the body. "The brain boys will love to get their hooks on this stuff."

Ross tried to put it around his own waist, but slender as he was, it would not close on him. Giving up, he clasped it about his wife.

Tarlroc watched them. He had not spoken before, but now he touched the dead Baldy with the toe of his boot. "So demons are flesh and blood after all."

His eyes fixed the Terrans. "You are demons yourselves. You beat them with their own weapon." The Dominionite shuddered. "I know now that they had never truly tried with me before . . ."

"We're humans who fought to remain human," Ross responded quickly to cut off that potentially dangerous line of thought.

"Rossin, come over here, will you?"

Ross glanced in the direction of the archeologist. His voice dropped. "Eveleen, keep an eye on this pup while I find out what Gordon wants. I trust him about as far as a three-year-old could toss him." All I Zanthor had to do was slip away, drive off their deer, and head back to his own people to raise a hunt against them while they were trapped on foot and without supplies or support deep in Condor Hall territory.

"Will do," she responded. "I'm not inclined to turn my back on him, either."

Gordon Ashe was crouched beside the nearer of the two fallen pillars. "Take a look at this," he told the younger man.

Murdock whistled softly. A lot of repair and replacement work still remained to be done, but enough had been completed for him to identify what he was seeing. "The makings of an old Model 1B time grid!"

His partner nodded. "They must've copied it straight from that installation they wrecked. No wonder they ran into trouble. That was set specifically for Terran conditions with each level leading directly to the next in our own history. It's almost incredible that they managed to bring as much through as they did before the whole thing blew up on them."

"That explains why they failed to act when things started to go badly for Zanthor. They didn't have the gear to take on a more active role, and he wouldn't give them the materials they needed to reestablish contact with their own time."

"That's the way I figure it."

"Why didn't their people come for them?"

"They still might, or maybe this was some sort of do-or-die experiment. I'd guess the latter since they were left to their own devices for so long."

"They never seemed to take an interest in time travel," Ross ventured, "otherwise they'd have done it long before we got into the act and probably made sure that we wouldn't."

"Let's hope that doesn't change . . ."

"Down!"

Murdock dove behind the pillar, dragging his partner with him, as a fury of blue light ripped through the space the two Terrans had occupied a moment before.

The partisan leader swore. The fifth Baldy! Like a damn fool, he had forgotten him, and now they would all pay for his failure. This one seemed to recognize his associates' error. He had come in with his laser, and the humans were no more than fixed targets in this open place. The spacer was not even bothering to conceal himself. He knew he would fry them all before they could so much as raise their bows.

Suddenly, Tarlroc I Zanthor sprang. The laser discharged, caught him squarely in the trunk, but momentum carried him forward. The Dominionite struck the blue-clad figure, his hands closing over the starman's throat even as he bore him to the ground.

The weapon fired again, striking at point-blank range. I Zanthor's body jerked and stiffened, but his fingers only tightened under the lash of the shock.

It was over by the time the Terrans reached the pair. Even then, Tarlroc's hands retained their hold. Ross turned him clumsily despite that, endeavoring to be as gentle as possible.

The Dominionite's eyes flickered open. Murdock felt sick. There seemed to be nothing left of him, and he was still alive . . .

"The demon?" I Zanthor's lips formed the words. No sound came.

"Dead. You got him."

A grotesque shadow of a smile. "I avenged . . ."

He was gone. The Time Agent wrenched himself to his feet and quickly crossed the clearing to distance himself from his comrades.

They left him be for a few moments, then Ashe joined him. "Ross?"

"A brave devil in the end."

"Yes."

Murdock turned to look at the most recent scene of carnage on the battlefield. His mouth twisted. "He was me," he said tightly. "If the Project hadn't grabbed me, or if I'd made a few wrong decisions at the start . . ."

Gordon looked closely at him. He took a deep breath. "Don't flatter yourself, my friend. You were a real little punk, right enough, and far too smart for your own good, but as a budding villain, you were never even in the same universe as I Zanthor. He lacked the experience and maybe the talent to put his potential into action, but otherwise he was of one cut with his father. You're capable of hate, but not indifference, nor, I think, of cruelty."

The younger man gripped himself. The Baldies were finished, for this round at any rate, but he and his companions were still three partisans alone in enemy country. "Are we about done here?"

"I'd like to check out these domes. After that, we'll have to grab whatever we can carry and torch the rest." The archeologist sighed. "A lot of folks back on the Project are going to be very disappointed, but we can't risk leaving anything that might be of use either to our star-roving acquaintances or to Condor Hall."

30

THE WAR DID not end immediately, but Condor Hall's fall was assured by the slaying of its Ton. Neither of Zanthor I Yoroc's remaining sons nor any of the mercenary commanders he had hired had the force of personality necessary to bind the rest to him, and none was strong enough to seize control by force of arms, thus reducing the invading front to several small, distinct armies, each only uncertainly bound to the others.

They continued to stand together, for only thus could they hope, as they at first did, to salvage anything out of what would otherwise be a totally disastrous campaign, but the sense of disorganization in their leadership did nothing to reassure or inspire troops already worn and discouraged after a winter of great cold and lean supplies, and the hard-pressing Confederates gained steadily against them.

The partisans continued to ride and fight, albeit not so frequently now, for while the front was still situated beyond the Corridor, there would be enemy activity in the lowlands.

That need would soon be lifted from them. It was but a matter of time, a few weeks at most, before Condor Hall itself became the battlefield, bringing home at last some of the horror its legions had carried to so many of its erstwhile neighbors.

Eveleen perched herself on the end of Ross's desk. "Luroc reports that the Tons are hotly discussing the division of spoil," she said to draw him out, although he, of course, was better aware of that fact than was she.

"They'd do better to wait until it's won."

She smiled. That was the response she should have expected from him.

Her eyes darkened. "Do you believe they'll honor their promises to us?" she asked him abruptly. "We're numerically much weaker than the least of them."

"They'll give us our due. Ton I Carlroc and most of those with him aren't men to violate their word, given or implied, and we have firm oaths from them."

"Most, but not all," the woman observed. "According to you, I Loran doesn't trust some of them."

"Probably with excellent reason from what I've seen of them, but don't worry. They'll walk the line. They know that Jeran A Murdoc'll squash them otherwise, even if their compatriots don't. Mercenaries take a very dim view of having any of their own kind cheated out of rightly won spoil since that would be a rather bad precedent to have established. Luroc's made it clear more than once that I'm to come into a good part of anything Sapphirehold gains."

The woman sighed in relief. "I'm glad to hear that. I was afraid we'd have to face further danger at the hands of our present allies once Condor Hall at last yields."

"Don't you trust anyone, Eveleeni EA Riordan?" Ross asked in some amusement.

"Given Terra's history, no, I don't," she responded curtly.

Eveleen smiled softly, her former humor forgotten even as it had been vented. "Plans are already being made for rebuilding the village and then the keep. That'll be both strong and fair when it's complete, better than the old one was and lots more comfortable."

"A joy to behold, I'm sure," he responded sarcastically.

His voice had become rough, almost angry. She looked at him in surprise, but the man made no answer to her unspoken question. He came to his feet and strode away from the desk to stand staring out the window.

She went to him. "Ross, don't you want to see a normal lifeway resumed here?"

"Of course, I do. You know that."

"What's wrong, then?" she pleaded. "You've been shadowed so often these last weeks, when the rest of us are growing ever more hopeful."

He looked at her, through her. "A failure of nerve, Lieutenant," he responded at last. "Only that."

Suddenly, he whirled toward the door. "Ride with me!"

The woman followed him. The partisans always kept springdeer saddled and at ready, and she raced for the place where hers was tethered, whispering a prayer of gratitude that it was yet early enough in the day that Spark would be her mount. No other had a hope of keeping pace with Firehand's doe if he drove her hard. Murdock was waiting for her now at the edge of the camp, but she doubted he would continue to do so once she was actually mounted.

Ashe had seen his partner cast himself into the saddle and hurried toward him. That some deep trouble was on him would have been patent even to one knowing him far less well.

Eveleen stopped him with a firm shake of her head as she swung herself onto her buck's back. Ross would never speak if two of them were present. She was unsure of her own ability to win confidence from him, although he had asked her to come with him and she could already make a pretty good guess as to the whip lashing him. Ross Murdock had to decide, and decide soon, whether to cast his lot with this Dominion of the past where he had proven he could work and rise far or return to Terra and the Project. This was not Karara's case. Murdock had not been altered. He had merely expanded, become aware of new potential, but the difficulty of the choice he faced was in no way lessened by that growth in self and knowledge.

Once he saw that his wife was mounted and prepared to follow him, Ross turned Lady Gay toward the trees and gave her the command for speed, as if flight could free him of that which was driving him, sunder his weakness from him.

The man did not draw rein or slacken pace until he came to that high place where he and Eveleen had stood together so many months before. He dismounted there and waited for her on the crest.

The world below and around him was wonderful with the gentle sunlight and soft, pale greens of a still young spring, but no trace of its joy touched him.

He heard the weapons expert's buck approach and halt near Lady Gay but did not turn to watch her.

He felt rather than saw her come up beside him.

Eveleen waited quietly for some seconds to give him an opportunity to collect himself, but he seemed unable to begin.

"Ross," she said softly in the end, "please let me try to help. I can't bear to see you torturing yourself like this."

He did not respond at first but finally shrugged. "As I told you before, I thought I had a proper spine. It appears I don't."

"Ross . . ."

He turned to her. "When we were here the last time, I asked you to stay with me."

"Yes. Now you don't want to remain?"

His eyes closed. "Heart, mind, and soul!" He pressed the fingers of his hands against the lids until the pressure became painful. "It's Sapphirehold that I want, Eveleen, and I can't have that. What I said to Allran was right. I am a mercenary, and soon there'll be nothing more for me to do here, no place for me."

Suddenly, the too-bright eyes fixed on her. "You knew it'd be like this, or Gordon did?"

Her head lowered. "If it was Sapphirehold itself and not Dominion in general that was drawing you, yes. We were hoping for the last, Ross. Both of us wanted you to be spared learning that part of a mercenary's existence, at least for a while."

Her eyes raised again and met his. "You can still make it in that work. You're good, and with any kind of luck at all, you'd win a Commandant's rank in a very few years."

His mouth twisted. "I find something basically unappealing about battering my fellow creatures for fun and profit." He scowled. "I seem to require a genuine purpose for what I do."

Murdock shrugged. "I couldn't stay anyway. I blew it, or we blew it, here, where folks were sympathetic to us. It'd happen again, and maybe Terra'd get wiped out as a result. We'd most likely disappear ourselves at that point, and everything we'd managed to accomplish thus far would probably be undone as well."

Ross sighed deeply. "No, Eveleeni EA Riordan," he said wearily, purposely stressing the Dominionite version of her name. "It's back to Terra and no rank or reputation for both of us. I think I've known that for a long time and just haven't had the guts to face it."

The Time Agent's eyes were dark, somber. He had surrendered the land and the place in it that he loved, and soon he would probably lose the rest as well.

There was no point in postponing that break if it must come. "Does our relationship still stand?" he demanded bluntly.

"What the hell do you think I am, Ross Murdock?" the woman flared, fury blazing from voice, face, and body in equal measure.

"I don't think you're a fool," he snapped coolly. "We could've made it big here, really carved out something for ourselves. That won't be true back home. Plain Ross Murdock's no prize, and I just want it clear that you've got an out. I won't try to chain you . . ."

"I fell in love with 'plain Ross Murdock' long before Firehand raised his head. . . . Or maybe you're the one who's thinking he hasn't made so marvelous a match. I won't bring you any great glory or fatten your bank account on Terra, either."

"No!"

His anger was sufficient rebuttal to that fear, and Eveleen's eyes slitted as her lips curved into a hunter's smile. "I'm so far from wanting out of our partnership, my Dear, that I've got every intention of redoing the ceremony according to Terran specifications as soon as I can arrange to have it performed."

"You what?"

The woman's face remained impassive for several seconds, then she took pity on him and laughed softly. "No standing at the altar rail dressed like an undertaker," she promised, "but the church service is important, and so's the presence of my father and brother. . . . Ross?"

Murdock knew he would agree. This really did mean a great deal to her. Hell, he would have given in had she asked for the whole show. "Whatever you want, Lieutenant. I don't mind the idea of showing off that I've won a most beautiful woman."

Murdock kissed her softly, then turned toward their mounts. "We'd best be getting back. There's a lot to be done yet before we have to call for a pickup."

The three months that followed passed in a blur of activity, but at last, Ross Murdock stood once more on the narrow crest. The heart in him felt dead and heavy enough to drag him down to the planet's core. Soon now, the chopper would come, and he would lose this beauty, lose everything it represented, for all the rest of his life.

Gordon was beside him. He said nothing, but his hand rested on his friend's shoulder, its pressure firm and warm.

"I'm glad I spoke up for Karara," the younger man said suddenly.

"She was lucky." Ashe's eyes rested on him. "I am, too, I guess. I'm deeply sorry this didn't work out for you, Ross, but I value our friendship. I didn't want to lose it."

The other forced the shadow of a smile. "Breaking in a new partner has to be a pain."

"A royal pain. . . . I'd have missed Eveleen, too. She'll be one major asset to our team in the future."

Gordon caught his sharp look. "I doubt she'll be sent back to the classroom. She's too good."

Murdock glanced downslope to the place where his wife was waiting. She had not been sure enough of her control following their parting with Luroc I Loran and their springdeer to stay with her comrades.

His eyes closed. That severing had been as painful as the wound that had so nearly finished him . . .

The Ton of Sapphirehold alone had been told of the off-worlders' imminent departure and had insisted on accompanying them most of the way to the rise, as far as they dared permit him to come. When he had turned back, he had taken the mounts who had served them so well, promising that all three would be left to run free with the breeding herd, never again to be brought by human-kind into danger and certainly never to be set to heavy labor. They, too, had served Sapphirehold with uncommon valor, and the domain was prepared to honor them for it even if it was to be prevented from honoring those they had so often borne.

Ross's head lifted sharply. There was a sound, distant yet but clear, in Dominion's still air.

Grief twisted in him, so sharp that he feared for a moment that he would not be able to master it. He turned to the archeologist in desperation. "It'll be just a quick jump once we reach the gate, won't it, only a shot to our own time and then aboard ship and home? We won't have to stay there?"

"Don't you want to know if we succeeded?" Ashe asked in surprise.

"We'll be told that. —This is the Dominion I want to remember, not a tamed, citified, modern planet with Luroc, Allran, and all the others so long dust that not even a memory of them remains, as if they had never lived at all."

Gordon looked closely, carefully, at him. "Yes," he said quietly. "I agree with you. I'll see that it's arranged."

31

THE TIME AGENTS stepped through the gate into the age in which they had been born.

They found themselves inside a building of some sort. Ross resolutely turned toward the door but then stopped, as if frozen or held by some powerful compulsion. "We—I have to go there," he said abruptly, "to Sapphirehold or what used to be Sapphirehold."

Gordon looked sharply at him. "You said . . ."

"I know, but if I don't make myself see it, I'll be running, and I'll spend the rest of my life running." He hesitated. "Do you think they'll let us?"

"You heard the pilot. We managed to save the whole damn planet. I doubt the brass here'll be too slow in granting us a simple request like that. . . . Through the door with you, Firehand! We'll find out in a few minutes."

The archeologist sighed as Eveleen's fingers caught his arm, staying him. She looked as if she could cheerfully murder him.

"Gordon," she hissed.

"He's right, Eveleen. He'll do it anyway. He has to do it, and if we try to block him, he won't see us as being there for him if he needs us."

"We'd both better start praying, then, hard, Gordon O Ashean. I don't want to see Ross ripped open."

"Nor do I, Lieutenant."

* * *

Murdock shut his eyes. Their copter was completely closed, and he had no way of seeing the countryside over which they were flying.

The combination space and surplanetary port from which they had lifted appeared to be part of an urban area, but he understood that this modern Dominion still retained a great deal of cultivated and undamaged land as well. Which one or what combination characterized the once-embattled island, he had not been able to nerve himself to ask.

Eveleen's hand squeezed into his, and Ashe moved a little closer on Ross's other side so that their shoulders met in a silent declaration of support. For a moment, the fog of his dread lightened. They were doing their best for him, doing all that could be done. Fate and time had taken the rest of it out of their hands.

What if it was gone, he wondered in despair, the very land as well as the ancient, long-superceded political division? He swallowed hard. The fact that Dominion of Virgin lived was their victory. Intellectually, he accepted that, but it was not all of Dominion that had taken his heart, just one small, exquisite part of her. One small part as it had been distant millennia ago . . .

His muscles tensed. There was a change in the motion of the chopper. They were beginning to descend.

Eveleen followed Ross through the narrow door space. The machine had brought them where they had requested to come but had set down at the base of the rise rather than at its summit to avoid the never-ending sweep of the wind rushing over it. That much, at least, remained constant with the conditions they remembered from the past.

They started to climb, Murdock first, his companions a few steps behind him. The grade itself, the vegetation around them, did not seem terribly alien, and the weapons expert gathered herself in one fierce prayer, one all-consuming hope, that the world soon to meet their eyes would prove as little jarring. It would not be the same. That, no one could expect, but, Lord of Time, let it be whole.

Let it be alive. This man of hers must always push himself, punish himself, to the end. Gordon was right. He had to do this, but if he found desolation or degradation only, she feared it would break something within him, a core part of his fine spirit and much, the best, of his heart.

They mounted the crest. Ross Murdock looked upon the scene he had watched with such infinite anguish both scant hours and a near eternity ago.

A sharp breath that was more than half sob rose to close his throat. Time had changed a little of what lay below, humanity a great deal more, but this realm still stood erect, unbroken, and in its essence unravaged.

He blinked misting eyes, trying to clear them and at the same time conceal his need to do so.

It might only have been that his vision was blurred, yet for an instant, perhaps a second or two, another landscape veiled the one of the present age. Ross's hand, the left, went out to it without conscious command from his mind. The scarred fingers curved, as if he would draw what he saw there to him.

"This land," he said in a voice that was no more than a whisper. "It is mine!"

His head raised. He had spoken the truth, affirmed the truth. What now lay in his body's and in his soul's eyes was his and would be his forever.

32

R OSS EXAMINED THE shelves covering the walls with satisfaction. Eveleen and he had taken the two-bedroom suite, and
this room was going to house the books they both would be
moving into it, plus those he knew would be added as time went
on. Some of the odd bits of knowledge he had picked up in the
course of his seemingly random program of reading had proven
useful on Dominion, and he doubted either he or the weapons
expert would slow down on their unofficial research into topics of
interest to them in the future.

As if in response to some mental call, the door opened, and
Eveleen Riordan came in. She was still wearing her cream-white
suit and looked stunningly beautiful despite her long, busy day.

"I thought I'd find you here," she said. "We'll start filling those
shelves tomorrow. There's a lot to be done in these two weeks
Kilgarries kindly gave us off."

"Kindly? We're entitled to a furlough."

"Well, we're not really entitled to quarters this spacious, so we
can thank the Major for that at least."

"With so pretty a bride, how could he refuse us a decent
wedding present?" he countered.

Murdock laughed softly, to himself. Half the men on the Project
were kicking themselves right now. Eveleen's abilities and aloof-
ness had effectively blinded the lot of them to much of the rest of
what she was, even as he himself had been blinded. Now that he
had made his move, his comrades could all see this aspect of her,

and he enjoyed their envious looks every bit as much as he had imagined he would.

"Speaking of wedding presents," the woman said, "here's my offering."

Ross took the long, narrow package she was holding from her. It was neatly and appropriately wrapped. He shook it and then started to slide the ribbon off. "Did you have to use so much tape?" he grumbled.

"It makes for tidier corners," she responded. "Hurry up, will you? I brought this all the way from Sapphirehold for you. I had it made specially."

Delaying no longer, he got the package open and the lid off the box inside. It held what looked like a leather belt, very thin and supple and extraordinarily wide but lacking any kind of buckle. He stared at it, puzzled for a moment, then his breath caught as he realized its purpose.

The woman nodded eagerly. "It'll cover your jeweled one so you can wear it and no one'll be the wiser. You couldn't go on keeping it under your clothes like some old-time monk's hair belt."

She looked up at him anxiously. "Do you like it, Ross? A watch would've been more traditional . . ."

Laughing, he took her in his arms. "I like it very much, Lieutenant EA Riordan. I just wish I'd shown equal imagination." She was wearing the pearls he had given her.

"I'm a very traditionally minded person," she responded, "about some things, anyway."

A buzz from the front door caused them to draw apart. "It's open!" Murdock called out.

A few moments later, Gordon Ashe joined them. He glanced admiringly at the shelves. "They won't be empty long," he commented.

"Not if we can help it," his partner agreed. The lightness had gone out of him. "What's the news, Gordon?"

They knew, of course, that Dominion of Virgin and her people did live. The almost deliriously enthusiastic reception of their colleagues had told them that, but Ashe had not delayed long in getting their party off-world once they had returned from the crest. There were so many things, subtle and gross, that might have altered with the change they had made in the planet's history. What if something, something terrible, had gone wrong as a result? Their people might not even have known to tell them then . . .

The other's broad smile put an end to that worry. "The only changes appear to be for the better, for the Dominionites at any rate. They're a feistier bunch now, with a lot more good old Terran spirit even if they're no more warlike than they were. They're also a damn harder crew to deal with in a trade situation. There'll have to be a great deal more give on our part before we get what we want out of them."

"I can't say I'm sorry to hear that," Eveleen remarked. "Our kind gets on better with those who can successfully stand up to us than with the totally meek and mild."

Ashe's eyes twinkled. "There's more, of personal interest to us."

Ross was willing to walk into that snare. "Such as?"

"We're fondly remembered, my Friends, the whole lot of us."

"What?" Ross demanded incredulously. "That's not possible, Gordon. It's been millennia . . ."

"Dominionites always were almost fanatical when it came to keeping records and histories. That didn't change when they came back, and they started doing it so early that we were still historical figures at the time, albeit already moving well toward the legendary. . . . Firehand, for example, though his accomplishments are realistically reported, is himself viewed as a sort of combination of Robin Hood and St. Michael the Archangel."

Eveleen broke into an open laugh at Ross's groan. "What about me?" she managed at last.

"You're Brunnhilde with a happy ending."

The woman made a face at him. "What of yourself, Healer O Ashean?"

"I am Merlin," he announced grandly, "except that I wave a scalpel and a bag of herbs instead of a wand."

"What about Luroc?" Ross asked quietly.

"A King Arthur whose Round Table never broke. . . . Zanthor I Yoroc doesn't come attached to horns, tail, and cloven hooves, but otherwise you can guess how he's recalled and regarded."

The archeologist sat down on a folding chair, the only piece of furniture in the room, apart from the waiting bookcases. "I'm afraid we can expect to take some ribbing on account of our new-found notoriety."

He looked from one to the other of them, suddenly deadly serious. "It also means that we're now considered the Project's top team, its star troubleshooters. When we get sent out again, it'll be on something big, and it'll be tough—if you two are still willing to go on with this."

Eveleen Riordan shrugged, an odd-looking gesture in the formal, very feminine wedding suit. "I'm not interested in going back to teaching school. I have certain talents, and I think they were meant to be put to use."

"Ross?" the older man asked gently. "None of our past missions together have been easy, and those to come are likely to be worse still. If you want out, no one'll hold it against you. You've paid your dues. In spades."

Murdock's eyes fixed on the empty shelves but stared beyond them. The terror of the run downriver, the searing of his hand, the never-ending dread of exile when that derelict had taken off with them aboard, the deadening trap of Hawaika's past, the raw, still-bleeding misery of his renunciation of Dominion, of Sapphirehold. . . . Aye, he had paid his dues.

A lot of others would have paid theirs if he had not.

His head turned once more. "I'm in, Gordon. I've got some pretty strange talents myself. Working for the Project seems like as good a way as any of putting them to use."

About the Authors

F OR OVER FIFTY years "one of the most distinguished living SF and fantasy writers" (*Booklist*), Andre Norton has been penning best-selling tales that earned her a unique place in the hearts and minds of readers. Honored as a Grand Master by both the Science Fiction Writers of America and the World Fantasy Convention, she has garnered millions of readers for her most famous series, the Witch World novels. These works and others, such as *Imperial Lady* (with Susan Shwartz), *Dare to Go A-Hunting*, and *The Jekyll Legacy* (with Robert Bloch), all Tor books, have made her "one of the most popular writers of our time" (*Publishers Weekly*). In addition to her novels, which number over forty works of SF and fantasy, she has recently created the *Tales of Witch World*. She lives in Winter Park, Florida.

P. M. Griffin has written a number of SF and fantasy novels, including *Seakeep* from *Storms of Victory* and *Falcon Hope* from *Flight of Vengeance*, the first and second books of *Witch World: The Turning*, and has contributed stories to two volumes in the *Tales of the Witch World* series. She is also the author of the *Star Commandos* adventure series. Her last collaboration with Andre Norton, *Redline the Stars*, was published last year by Tor books. She lives in New York City.